John W. Dean

Memoir of Rev. Michael Wigglesworth

author of The day of doom

John W. Dean

Memoir of Rev. Michael Wigglesworth
author of The day of doom

ISBN/EAN: 9783337388010

Printed in Europe, USA, Canada, Australia, Japan

Cover: Foto ©Andreas Hilbeck / pixelio.de

More available books at **www.hansebooks.com**

MEMOIR

OF

Rev. Michael Wigglesworth,

AUTHOR OF THE DAY OF DOOM.

BY

JOHN WARD DEAN.

SECOND EDITION.

ALBANY, N. Y. :
JOEL MUNSELL.
1871.

TO

WILLIAM REED DEANE, ESQ.,

OF

MANSFIELD, MASS.,

WITH WHOM THE WRITER HAS SPENT, IN FORMER YEARS, MANY
PLEASANT HOURS

IN

HISTORICAL AND LITERARY PURSUITS,

This Book is Inscribed.

PREFACE.

This memoir was originally prepared for the *New England Historical and Genealogical Register,* and was published in that periodical in April, 1863. The same type was used to print one hundred copies, in pamphlet form, for private distribution. The present edition is considerably enlarged.

The Appendix contains a brief autobiography, a collation of the different editions of his poems, and a catalogue of his library.

J. W. D.

Boston, Massachusetts.

MEMOIR

REV. MICHAEL WIGGLESWORTH.

———————•———————

A century ago, had it been asked what poem was most popular in New England, the answer probably would have been, *Wigglesworth's Day of Doom;* for Time that had then seen three generations of readers of this remarkable book pass away had not yet dimmed its popularity. It was still eagerly read from torn broadside or well-thumbed volume; it was still taught with the catechism to the child at the father's knee.[1]

True, a higher taste in poetry had been established here than was prevalent when the *Day of Doom* was written. The English poets were more generally

---

[1] Francis Jenks, Esq., in an article in the *Christian Examiner* for Nov. and Dec., 1828 (vol. VI, p. 537), speaks of the *Day of Doom* as: "A work which was taught our fathers with their Catechisms, and which many an aged person with whom we are acquainted can still repeat, though they may not have met with a copy since they

read, and some of our native bards had shown considerable ability in their metrical productions. The writings of the witty rivals, Mather Byles and Joseph Green, were then highly admired, and the *Choice* by Benjamin Church, was charming its readers by a smooth and flowing style. It requires no stretch of the imagination to suppose that the literati of Boston of that day preferred the polished strains of these writers to the religious rhymes of faithful Michael Wigglesworth. But the great body of the people of New England, and especially those who held fast to the faith of their fathers, were the sincere admirers of the bard of Malden, and delighted in his homely but descriptive and powerful language.

The popularity of Wigglesworth dated from the appearance of his poem, and had then been established for a full century. Expressing in earnest words the theology which they believed, and pic-

---

were in leading strings; a work that was hawked about the country printed on sheets like common ballads ; and, in fine, a work which fairly represents the prevailing theology of New England at the time it was written, and which Mather thought might ' perhaps find our children till the day [of doom] itself arrives.' "

turing in lively colors the terrors of the Judgment
Day and the awful wrath of an offended God, it
commended itself to those zealous Puritans who had
little taste for lofty rhyme or literary excellence.
The imaginative youth devoured its horrors with
avidity and shuddered at its fierce denunciations of
sin. In the darkness of night he saw its frightful
forms arise to threaten him with retribution till he
was driven to seek the ark of safety from the wrath
of Jehovah. For the last century, however, the
reputation of the *Day of Doom* has probably waned,
and few at the present day know it except by
reputation.[1]

The author of this book, whose wand has sum-
moned up such images of terror, was neither a cynic
nor a misanthrope, though sickness, which nourishes
and brings to light such dispositions where they
exist, had long been his companion. His attenuated
frame and feeble health were joined to genial
manners; and, though subject to fits of despond-
ency, he seems generally to have maintained a

[1] Since this was written, an edition of the *Day of Doom* has been
published at New York.

2

cheerful temper; for some of his friends, as he himself complains, would not believe that his illness
was real.[1] Frequent entries found in his common-
place book show that he had a meek disposition and
an humble estimate of his own talents and virtue,
and that he was sincerely grateful for the least
particle of praise or the least show of kindness.

Rev. Michael Wigglesworth was the son of
Edward Wigglesworth and was born October 18,
1631.[2] The only clues we have to his birthplace
are those which he himself furnishes in an autobiographic sketch still preserved in his own handwriting. He calls it "an ungodly place," and
informs us that the generality of the people there
rather derided than imitated the piety of his parents.
Probably all that he means is that the greater part
of the inhabitants were not Puritans. He tells us

---

[1] To the Christian Reader — lines prefixed to the *Day of Doom*.

[2] The month and day are obtained from Rev. Michael Wigglesworth's own memorandum, Oct. 18, 1669; and the year from his
gravestone, the title page of his funeral sermon and the diary of
Judge Sewall, of which the two former represent him to have
been in his 74th year, and the latter calls him 73 years and 8
months old when he died, June 10, 1705. He was really 73 years
7 months and 23 days old.

that a large portion of the place was consumed by fire after his parents had emigrated from it. Possibly we may at some time obtain information that will make these hints of service.[1]

There is some reason to think that he was probably from Yorkshire,[2] or at least that the family originated there. In this county the earliest mention of the name of Wigglesworth that I have met with occurs; and even at the present day it is seldom found elsewhere. In Whitaker's *History of Craven*, Yorkshire, Adam de Wigglesworth is mentioned among the monks of Fountains Abbey, which church

[1] Horace Day, Esq., of New Haven, Conn., soon after the publication of this memoir in the *Historical and Genealogical Register*, suggested to me that this place might be Hedon or Heydon near Hull in Yorkshire, a great portion of which was burnt in 1656; but John M. Bradbury, Esq., a descendant of Rev. Michael Wigglesworth, while in England, in 1869, wrote to the vicar of Hedon to have the registers examined. The vicar replied : " The clerk has made the search you asked for, but can find no trace of the name Wigglesworth."

[2] John M. Bradbury, Esq., before mentioned, who has made personal searches at London and in Yorkshire to ascertain the English pedigree of this family, wrote me from London, Eng., Oct. 11, 1869 : " Finding in the London Registry the wills of only one Wigglesworth family *out* of Yorkshire and that one just in the edge of it and within thirty miles of Wigglesworths *in* Yorkshire, I shall

was founded in 1206.[1]　We know that Michael had
relatives at, or in the vicinity of Gildersome, in the
West Riding of that county;[2] and the surname
Wigglesworth is still found in places in that vicinity.
In the Parish of Long Preston, in the same Riding
of Yorkshire, there is a township by this name;
and at Slaidburn, a few miles from that township,
a family of Wigglesworths has long been settled.
The living of Slaidburn was till recently in the gift of
a branch of the family residing in London.[3]　There
is a tombstone to the memory of Henry Wiggles-

---

read your cautious statement 'probably from Yorkshire' with a
strong superlative before the adverb."

[1] Letter of Rev. James Wiglesworth of Chickerell, Dorsetshire,
Eng., to Joel Munsell, Esq., of Albany, N. Y., dated Oct. 31, 1863.

[2] See letter of M. Middlebrook to Rev. Michael Wigglesworth,
dated April 6, 1657, vol. I, page 5, of the "*Eleer MSS.*," in the
library of the New England Historic Genealogical Society.　This
letter has been printed in full in the *Historical and Genealogical
Register*, vol. XI, page 110.　Some of the persons mentioned as relatives to Rev. Mr. Wigglesworth were such through his first wife
Mary, daughter of Humphrey Reyner of Rowley and niece of Rev.
John Reyner of Plymouth and Dover.　Perhaps all of them were so.

[3] Letter of Rev. James Wiglesworth, of Chickerell, Eng., before
quoted.　His uncle, the late Rev. Henry Wiglesworth, was rector of
Slaidburn.　The living in 1863, was in the gift of Mr. Jer. Wilkin-
son, of a family long resident in the place.

worth in the churchyard at Slaidburn dated in the
first half of the seventeenth century.

His parents, according to Mather, were "Eminently Religious," and had been "great Sufferers
for that which was then the *Cause of God* and of *New
England*." [1] He himself tells us that they "feared
the Lord greatly from their youth;" but met with
opposition and persecution for their religion, "because they went from their own Parish church to hear
the Word and receive the Lord's Supper." They
therefore resolved "to pluck up their stakes and
remove themselves to New England. And accordingly they did so, leaving dear Relations, friends and
acquaintance: a new built house, a flourishing trade,
to expose themselves to the hazard of the seas, and
to the distressing difficulties of a howling wilderness,
that they might enjoy liberty of conscience and
Christ in his ordinances." The resolute Puritans of
the class to which Edward Wigglesworth belonged,
whose devotion to principle and love of God led
them with their families to this continent, here to
found an asylum where they and their brethren and

---

[1] *Funeral Sermon*, p. 22.

posterity could enjoy their religion without molest-
ation, have often been eulogized by orators and
poets, and certainly their sacrifices for principle are
deserving of all the eulogy bestowed upon them. In
expatriating themselves from their English homes
to this "wilderness world" they separated themselves from their friends and kindred in a manner
that in these days, when the telegraph and steam
are annihilating time and space, cannot be realized.
Here they suffered the severe hardships of a rigorous
climate and the fearful dangers from savage tribes
around them, while uniting to build up villages
which are now cities, and which still retain some of
the characteristics of their Puritan founders.

Edward Wigglesworth and his family arrived at
Charlestown,[1] between the 7th of August and the
15th of September, 1638,[2] probably in the latter part

---

[1] *Autobiography of Rev. Michael Wigglesworth.* See Appendix,
No. I.

[2] Rev. Michael Wigglesworth in his *Autobiography* says that he
was not quite seven years old when they arrived, consequently their
arrival was previous to October 18, 1638, though not a great while
before that date. He also states that, after about seven weeks stay
at Charlestown, they removed to New Haven, and that their removal
was in the month of October. Their stay could not have been

of August in that year.[1]   They remained at Charlestown till the following October ; and then sailed in
a vessel for New Haven.[2]   There is scarcely a doubt
that they were at Charlestown, September 14, 1638,
when Rev. John Harvard died at that place.   Little
I presume did Mr. Wigglesworth think that his
young son, Michael, who it is possible may have
attended the funeral of that clergyman, would be
benefited by the property which he left, as proved
to be the case ; for Harvard left a bequest to the
college at Cambridge, where Michael was subsequently educated.

During their passage to New Haven, the vessel
encountered a storm and ran ashore, but where we
are not informed.[3]   It is possible that this was one

---

longer than seven weeks and six days, nor their removal earlier than
October 1 ; therefore their arrival was not before the 7th of August.
Their stay could not have been less than six weeks and four days,
nor their removal later than October 31 ; therefore their arrival was
not after the 15th of September.

[1] If the vessel in which the family sailed was one of those mentioned by Winthrop as cast away at Aquiday on the 14th or 15th
of October, there is no doubt of it.

[2] *Autobiography of Rev. M. Wigglesworth.*

[3] *Ibid.*

of the " two vessels bound for Quinnipiack " which,
according to Winthrop, " were cast away at Aquiday " in a severe north-east storm which began on
the night of the 14th of October and continued the
next day. " So great a tempest of wind and snow,"
he writes, " had not been since our time." He adds
that the people in both vessels were saved.[1]
Against this suggestion, it may be urged that the
vessel in which the Wigglesworth family sailed was
able, after a short detention, to finish her voyage,
whereas Winthrop gives the impression though he
may not have intended to do so, that the vessels
mentioned by him were lost.

The winter that followed their arrival in New
Haven, the family lived in a cellar, partly under
ground, covered with earth. On one occasion, the
rain broke into the cellar; and Michael, who was
then asleep in bed, was so drenched with water that
a severe fit of sickness ensued.[2]

The location of Mr. Wigglesworth's house in New
Haven, I have not been able to ascertain. In

---

[1] *Savage's Winthrop*, vol. 1, 1st ed., pp. 286-7 ; 2d ed., pp. 344-5.
[2] *Rev. M. Wigglesworth's Autobiography.*

March, 1647 – 8, he conveyed to Adam Nicholls, six
acres of land in the Yorkshire quarter,[1] but this
estate does not appear to have been his homestead.[2]
The Yorkshire quarter, also called Mr. Evance's
quarter[3] was one of five portions into which the
town was divided.[4] There was also a Hertfordshire
quarter.[5]

The Yorkshire men are mentioned at New Haven
as early as Nov. 25, 1639.[6] I think it not unlikely
that they may have been a part of the company
from Yorkshire that came with Rev. Ezekiel
Rogers, and subsequently settled at Rowley. Some
of this company are known to have gone to New
Haven in the autumn of 1638.[7] Though Mr.
Rogers sent a pinnace, the next year, to bring them
back, yet the New Haven people were reluctant
to lose them,[8] and some of them may have been
prevailed upon to take up their residence there.

---

[1] *New Haven Colonial Records,* vol. 1, p. 370.   [2] *Ibid.*   [3] *Ibid.,* p. 196,
[4] They were called usually, Mr. Davenport's, Mr. Eaton's, Mr.
Robert Newman's, Mr. Tenche's, and Mr. Evance's quarters.—
Ibid., p. 194.   [5] *Ibid.,* p. 24.   [6] *Ibid.,* p. 25.
[7] *Savage's Winthrop,* vol. 1, 1st ed., p. 294 ; 2d ed., p. 354.
[8] *Ibid.,* 1st ed., p. 294 ; 2d ed., p. 355.

It is extremely probable that Mr. Wigglesworth came to New England with Mr. Rogers. They arrived near if not at, the same time, Mr. Rogers having landed here in the summer of 1638,[1] and Mr. Wigglesworth late in that summer or early in the autumn. Besides, Mr. Wigglesworth went to New Haven the same fall that a portion of Mr. Rogers's company did. If he came in that company, a reason is furnished why his son went to so great a distance as Rowley to find a wife when he was first married.

Rev. Mr. Rogers had been settled at Rowley in Yorkshire, and his company was chiefly, if not entirely, from that county. The ships in which they came were brought for him from London to Hull where he and his people embarked for New England.[2] His company consisted according to Winthrop of " some twenty families, godly men and most of them of good estate."[3] His relative,

---

[1] *Savage's Winthrop*, vol. I, 1st ed., p. 278; 2d ed., p. 335.

[2] *Mather's Magnalia*, bk. III, ch. XIII, sect. 8.

[3] *Savage's Winthrop*, vol. 1, 1st ed., p. 294; 2d ed., p. 354; Johnson's number of about three score families at Rowley, probably refers to a later date. See *Wonder Working Providence*, p. 130.

Rev. Nathaniel Rogers, states the number of persons
to have been about two hundred.[1] He had been
urged to settle at New Haven,[2] and at first was favor-
ably disposed towards the proposition ;[3] but he finally
decided to begin a new plantation near his step
brother, Rev. Nathaniel Ward, and his cousin Rev.
Nathaniel Rogers, both of whom resided at Ipswich.

The summer after Mr. Wigglesworth's arrival at
New Haven, he sent his son Michael, then a lad less
than eight years old, to the school of Master Ezekiel
Cheever. Mr. Cheever, who was a young man but
twenty-three years of age and recently married,
taught school in his own house at New Haven.
He was afterwards a schoolmaster in Ipswich,
Charlestown, and Boston, at the last of which places,
nearly seventy years after young Wigglesworth
became his pupil, he ended his days.[4] He was
famous for the length of time spent in his pro-

---

[1] *Historical Magazine,* vol. I, p. 148.

[2] *Mather's Magnalia,* and *Savage's Winthrop, ubi supra.*

[3] *Savage's Winthrop, ubi supra.*

[4] His former pupil, Rev. Cotton Mather, preached his funeral
sermon which was printed by John Allen at Boston in 1708, the
year of his death, under the title, *Corderius Americanus.* In 1828,

fession and also for the number and celebrity of his
scholars. Under his instruction, Michael spent a
year or two, and "began to make Latin and to get
forward apace;" but his father being afflicted with
a severe lameness, he was taken from school to
assist him in his labors.[1]

This lameness of Mr. Wigglesworth was brought
on in the second or third winter of his residence in
this country, probably the third, that is the winter
of 1640–1. In lifting, on a very cold day, he
strained himself, in his back, and took a cold upon it.
Though he felt no pain at the time, a weakness soon
appeared that kept him from his labor and continued
till his death twelve or thirteen years after this.[2]

When Michael was in his fourteenth year, his
father, he tells us, considering him unfit for agri-

---

it was reprinted also at Boston by Dutton & Wentworth, with the
addition of *A Selection from the Poems of Mr. Cheever's Manuscripts.* A memoir of him was published in Barnard's *American
Journal of Education* for March, 1856 (pp. 297, 314), and was reprinted with additions in a pamphlet of thirty-two pages.

[1] *Autobiography.*

[2] Letter of Edward Wigglesworth, *Mass. Hist. Coll.*, vol. XXIX,
pp. 296–7, and *Autobiography of Michael Wigglesworth,* before
quoted.

cultural pursuits, and besides having, from his
infancy intended that he should receive a liberal
education, again sent him to school.[1] I presume
that this was in the autumn of 1644. He had then
spent three or four years away from school, and had
forgotten nearly all he had learned of the Latin
language. He felt therefore little disposition for
study; but as in duty bound he yielded obedience
to the will of his father and applied himself to his
studies. He did this under great disadvantage and
discouragement, for many who had been below him
in acquirements had outstripped him. In a little
time, however, he overcame these difficulties. By
degrees, his studies became easier to him, so that
he soon recovered what he had lost and made new
advances in knowledge. This progress was so
rapid that in two years and three-quarters he was
pronounced fit to enter college. Accordingly he
was sent to Cambridge, "among strangers" and "far
from parents and acquaintances," to use his own
pathetic language.[2] I presume he was admitted to

[1] *Autobiography of M. Wigglesworth.*   [2] *Ibid.*

college in the summer of 1647.[1] In that year the fifth class was graduated; and the whole number that had taken their first degree there was then but thirty-one.

"It was an act of great self denial in my father," he writes, " that notwithstanding his own lameness and great weakness of body, which required the service and helpfulness of a son, and having but one son to be the staff of his age and supporter of his weakness, he would yet, for my good, be content to deny himself that comfort and assistance I might have lent him. It was also an evident proof of a strong faith in him, in that he durst adventure to send me to the colledge, though his estate was but small and little enough to maintain himself and his small family left at home. And God let him live to see how acceptable to himself this service was in giving up his only son to the Lord and bringing him up to learning; especially the lively actings of his faith and self denial herein. For first, notwith-

---

[1] Rev. Simon Bradstreet, who entered Harvard College in 1656, records that he was " admitted to the university " June 25, of that year. See *Hist. and Gen. Register*, vol. IX, p. 118.

standing his great weakness of body, yet he lived til
I was so far brought up as that I was called to be a
Fellow of the colledge, and improved in public service there, and until I had preached several times; yea
and more then so, he lived to see and hear what God
had done for my soul in turning me from darkness to
light and from the power of Sathan unto God, which
filled his heart ful of joy and thankfulness beyond
what can be expressed.   And for his outward estate,
that was so far from being sunk by what he had spent
from yeer to yeer upon my education, that in six years
time it was plainly doubled, which himself took great
notice of, and spake of it to myself and others, to the
praise of God, with admiration and thankfulness."[1]

When Michael Wigglesworth entered Harvard
College, Rev. Henry Dunster, its first president, had
been at the head of the institution for seven years,
and had raised it from the low state in which it was
left by his predecessor, Rev. Nathaniel Eaton,[2] to

---

[1] *Autobiography.*

[2] Mr. Eaton was not styled president; but he was at the head of
the college.   See an article by Hon. Timothy Farrar, LL.D., in the
Historical and Genealogical Register, vol. IX, p. 269.

one of respectability and efficiency. Its prospects, however, even then, were not very flattering; and it needed all the perseverance and energy of the president to overcome the difficulties that surrounded him. In that very year, Dunster states that the college building had become, owing to defects in its construction, decayed in its roof, walls and foundation; while its library was deficient in every department of learning, especially in physics, philosophy and mathematics.[1] Its funds and resources, also, were small and precarious.

Even the scholars whom New England had made sacrifices to instruct here in the higher branches of learning, were deserting her soil. "Of the *twenty* scholars, who had been graduated at the college prior to 1646, twelve had actually gone to Europe; all of whom found employment there, and eleven of them never returned to this country,"[2] It was

---

[1] Petition of Rev. Henry Dunster to the Commissioners of the United Colonies in the Acts of the Commissioners, printed in the *Records of Plymouth Colony*, vol. IX, pp. 93–5.

[2] *Quincy's History of Harvard University*, vol. I, p. 16. See also *Johnson's Wonder-working Providence*, p. 224.

not to be supposed that the colonists would long continue to give of their limited means for the purpose of raising up learned men, if their learning was to be used for the benefit of communities much more able to defray the expenses of their education. The evil likely to flow from this cause seems to have attracted the attention of the commissioners of the United Colonies,[1] as well as of the president of the college,[2] and their thoughts were directed to the providing of a way to avert it.

Rev. Mr. Dunster was eminently fitted for the office which he held. He was learned, conscientious, and entirely devoted to the interests of the institution; not only making urgent appeals to the people and government for aid, but giving of his own scanty substance to increase its means.[3] He was a graduate of the University of Cambridge,[4] and

---

[1] *Acts of the Commissioners of the United Colonies* in *Plymouth Colony Records*, edited by David Pulsifer, A.M., vol. IX, pp. 82 and 96.

[2] Petition of Rev. Henry Dunster in *Plymouth Colony Records*, vol. IX, p. 95.

[3] *Quincy's History of Harvard University*, vol. I, p. 15.

[4] *Massachusetts Historical Collections*, vol. XXVIII, p. 248.

4

was particularly skilled in the Hebrew language.[1]
Quincy, writing of him and his successor, the Rev.
Charles Chauncy, says, they were "learned beyond
the measure of their contemporaries; and probably,
in this respect, were surpassed by no one who has
since succeeded to their chair."[2] Under great
discouragements he labored to educate a race of
scholars for the benefit of the New World. His
success in making them good linguists may be
judged of by a fact which he communicated to
Christianus Ravius, professor of the oriental languages at London, in a letter written about the year
1649, namely, that some of his pupils could "with
ease dextrously translate Hebrew and Chaldee into
Greek."[3] The Syriac, as well as the Hebrew and
Chaldee languages were among the regular studies
of Harvard College.[4] To make the students pro-
ficients as linguists, the following rule had been

---

[1] *Mather's Magnalia*, bk. III, ch. XII.

[2] *Quincy's History of Harvard University*, vol I, p. 14.

[3] *Massachusetts Historical Collections*, vol. XXXI, p. 254.

[4] "The Times and Order of their Studies" at Harvard College,
printed in *New England's First Fruits*, London, 1643, p. 15; and reprinted in *Peirce's History of Harvard University*, App. pp. 6-7.

adopted : " The scholars shall never use their mother tongue, except that in public exercises of oratory or such like, they be called to make them in English."[1] This rule does not appear to have been in operation until after the first class was graduated, or at least it is not found in the code printed in 1643 in *New England's First Fruits.*[2]

It may assist us in judging of the attainments of Michael Wigglesworth, when he entered the college, to know that a candidate for admission was then required to be "able to read Tully or such like classical Latin author *extempore*, and make and speak true Latin, in verse and prose *suo* (*ut aiunt*) *Marte*, and decline perfectly the paradigm of nouns and verbs in Greek tongue."[3] Some of his college exercises are preserved, which show him to have

[1] *Laws, Liberties and Orders of Harvard College confirmed by the Overseers and the President of the College in the years* 1642, 1643, 1644, 1645 *and* 1646, printed in *Quincy's History of Harvard University*, vol. I, pp. 515–17.

[2] *New England's First Fruits*, pp. 13, 15 ; *Peirce's History of Harvard University*, App, pp. 4–6.

[3] *Laws, Liberties and Orders of Harvard College*, ubi supra, see also *New England's First Fruits*, p. 13.

been a careful and industrious student.[1] The two
higher classes at that time were required, whenever
called upon, to repeat publicly the sermons preached
in the hall;[2] and a great number of sermons,
delivered while he was at college, taken down by him
in short-hand, are preserved. The practice of taking
down sermons in short-hand was not new to him,
however; for some of those which he heard at New
Haven are found in the same volume.

"When I came first to the colledge," he states in
his *Autobiography*, "I had indeed enjoyed the benefit
of Religious and strict education, and God in his
mercy and pitty kept me from scandalous sins,
before I came thither and after I came there; but,
alas, I had a naughty vile heart, and was acted by
corrupt nature, and therefore could propound no
right and noble ends to myself, but acted from self
and for self. I was indeed studious, and strove to
outdoe my compeers; but it was for honor, and

---

[1] See his common-place books in the library of the *New England
Historic Genealogical Society.*

[2] *Laws, Liberties and Orders of Harvard College* in *Quincy's
History of Harvard University*, vol. I, p. 516.

applause, and preferment, and such poor beggarly
ends. Thus I had my ends, and God had his ends,
far differing from mine ; yet it pleased him to bless my
studies, and to make me to grow in knowledge both
in the tongues and inferior arts, and also in Divinity.
But when I had been there about three years and a
half, God, in his love and pitty to my soul, wrought
a great change in me, both in heart and life, and
from that time forward I learnt to study with God
and for God. And whereas before that, I had
thoughts of applying myself to the study and practice
of physick, I wholly laid aside those thoughts, and
did chuse to serve Christ in the work of the ministry,
if he would please to fit me for it, and to accept of
my service in that great work."

His conversion may have been owing to the
preaching of the excellent Jonathan Mitchell, who
had been his tutor in college, but who had lately
been settled as pastor of the church at Cambridge.
Rev. Mr. Mitchell was a native of Yorkshire — the
county in which I have supposed Wigglesworth
himself to have been born — and was graduated at
Harvard College in 1647, the year that his pupil

probably entered it. The friendship between tutor and pupil, begun within the college walls, was not interrupted when the latter removed to the neighboring town of Malden, and the commendatory lines, signed J. Mitchell, prefixed to the *Day of Doom*, if written by the former,[1] evince a warm appreciation of the talents and worth of his pupil.

In 1651, he was graduated. The commencement exercises took place on Tuesday, August 12, at

---

[1] On the title page of the 1751 edition of the *Day of Doom*, the writer is called Rev. *John* Mitchell. I do not attach much importance to an anonymous statement like this, though it may be correct. I have met with no Rev. John Mitchell in this country, at so early a date as the lines were printed ; but as there is no proof that the writer was a resident of New England, this is not conclusive that his Christian name was not John. In fact one expression favors the idea that the writer resided abroad. He says :

"In *those* vast woods a Christian Poet Sings."

A resident would be likely to say, " *these* vast woods ;" unless the marks of parenthesis are wrongly placed, and the writer meant,

"Those vast woods, where whilom Heathen wild were only found."

The following line :

"From this Eater comes some Meat,"

if it refers to Wigglesworth's poem called *Meat out of the Eater*, would tell against the idea that Rev. Jonathan Mitchell was the author, for he died July 9, 1668, and *Meat out of the Eater* was not

which he, and nine other students, took the degree
of Bachelor of Arts.[1] The exercises probably did
not materially differ from those in 1642, when the
first class was graduated, of which Gov. Winthrop
and some ministers of the colony, gave the following
account in a letter, sent to England, dated at " Boston
in New England, September the 26th, 1642.

  " The students of the first classis that have beene
these foure yeeres trained up in University learning

finished till October 31, 1669, more than a year afterwards.   It is
barely possible that Mr.Mitchell may have seen the unfinished manuscript before his death, for under date of Sept. 17, 1669, Wigglesworth records that he had been " long employed " upon the work.

  The metaphor, referring to Samson's riddle, would be a very
natural one in this connection, even before the author of the *Day
of Doom* had conceived the idea of his other poem.   He uses it
himself, some years before the death of Mitchell.   After relating
the providence of God to him, after his return from Bermuda in
1664, he utters this exclamation : " He brings meat out of the Eater ;
O blessed be thy gracious and holy name, most dear Father !"

  Perhaps, even then he had conceived the idea of his poem, and
had conversed with his former tutor and pastor upon it.

  [1] " The number of students is much encreased of late, so that the
present year, 1651, on the twelfth of the sixth moneth, ten of them
took the degree of Batchelors of Art, among whom the Sea-born
son of Mr. Iohn Cotton was one."— *Johnson's Wonder-Working Providence*, p. 166.   For the names of the graduates, see *Catalogus
Universitatis Harvardiana*, p. 2.

(for the ripening in the knowledge of the tongues, and arts) and are approved for their manners, as they have kept their publick Acts in former yeares, ourselves being present at them ; so have they lately kept two solemn Acts for their Commencement, when the Governor, Magistrates, and the Ministers from all parts, with all sorts of Schollars, and others in great numbers were present, and did heare their exercises ; which were Latine and Greeke Orations, and Declamations, and Hebrew Analysis, Grammaticall, Logicall, and Rhetoricall of the Psalms : And their answers and disputations in Logicall, Ethicall, Physicall, and Metaphysicall questions ; and so were found worthy of the first degree (commonly called Batchelour) *pro more Academiarum in Anglia :* Being first presented by the President to the Magistrates and Ministers, and by him, upon their approbation, solemnly admitted unto the same degree, and a booke of arts delivered into each of their hands, and power given them to read Lectures in the hall upon any of the arts, when they shall be thereunto called, and a liberty of studying in the library."[1]

---

[1] *New England's First Fruits,* pp. 16, 17.

In the college catalogue, the name of Michael Wigglesworth stands at the head of his class. Peirce, in his *History of Harvard University*, states that he was so "placed from the rank of his family."[1] Mr. Sibley, the successor of Mr. Peirce as librarian of the University, concurs with his predecessor so far as to think that the principle upon which classes were then arranged was the social position of the parents. " The mode of arranging the early members of the Harvard classes," he writes to me, " was uniformly according to family rank and consequence. A great many elements were taken into account, and great bickerings followed. One of the heaviest punishments which could be inflicted was degradation of position; and it is from this cause that several graduates do not stand on the Triennial where they otherwise would. I have no doubt that this principle of arrangement was from the beginning."[2] The fact that the college rules, at that time, recognized the rank of the parents in the manner of addressing

[1] *P irce's History of Harvard University*, p. 150.
[2] *Manuscript Letter*, April 4, 1865. See also *Proceedings of the Massachusetts Historical Society*, 1864–5, pp. 32–7.

the students,[1] makes it reasonable to suppose that they also recognized it in placing them in the classes: especially, as it is well known that this was done in the next century down to the year 1773.[2]

Though hesitating to differ from Messrs. Peirce and Sibley upon a subject so familiar to them as the history and customs of Harvard College; yet in looking at this and some of the contemporary classes, I cannot help feeling a doubt, notwithstanding the fact before stated, whether social position was adopted so early as this, at college, as the standard of rank at graduation. Among the classmates of young Wigglesworth were some whose parents evidently held a higher position in society than his. Thomas Dudley was a son of Rev. Samuel Dudley, and the grandson of two governors[3] of the

---

[1] Every scholar shall be called by his surname only, till he is invested with his first degree, except he be a fellow commoner, or knight's eldest son, or of superior nobility.— Laws, etc., of Harvard College, in *Quincy's History of Harvard University*, vol. 1, p. 517.

[2] *Proceedings of Mass. Hist. Society*, 1864–5, pp. 32–7; Letter of Hon. Paine Wingate, Feb. 15, 1831, in *Peirce's History of Harvard University*, p. 308.

[3] Gov. Thomas Dudley and Gov. John Winthrop.

colony; Seaborn Cotton was a son of Rev. John
Cotton, teacher of the first church in Boston; and
Isaac and Ichabod Chauncy were sons of Rev.
Charles Chauncy, afterwards president of the
college. Here are four students whose parents held
positions of honor among the colonists and were
descended from the gentry of England; and they
are placed on the catalogue of the college below the
son of one whose name on the *New Haven Colonial
Records*, where it frequently occurs, is never found
with the honorary prefix of "Mr."[1] Is it likely
that all these young men forfeited their rank by
misconduct?

He was chosen a fellow of the college not long
after he was graduated; and was one of the earliest
members of the corporation chosen by the body
itself. The act incorporating the college, passed at
the May session of the General court in 1650, provided that the corporation should consist of seven

_____

[1] Judging by the records of New Haven Colony and other documents, I should say that Edward Wigglesworth held a middle place
in society, as to property and social consideration, being neither
among the highest class of the settlers, nor among the lowest.

persons, namely: a president, five fellows and a treasurer; and that Henry Dunster should be the first president, Samuel Mather, M.A., Samuel Danforth, M.A. Jonathan Mitchell, B.A., Comfort Starr, B.A., and Samuel Eaton, B.A., the five fellows, and that Thomas Danforth should be the treasurer. The corporation was empowered, with the consent of the overseers, to fill vacancies in its body.[1] In 1651, it is said that Samuel Danforth, who had been settled as a minister at Roxbury, had ceased to be a fellow ;[2] and we know that Samuel Mather, and Comfort Starr, had left New England. It was probably as the successor of one of these persons,. that Mr. Wigglesworth was chosen. He tells us in his autobiography that he was a Fellow before the death of his father, that is before October, 1653.

Most of the early fellows of the college, if not all, served as tutors there.[3] Mr. Wigglesworth

---

[1] *Records of the Massachusetts Colony*, vol. III, p. 195 ; vol. IV, part I, p. 13.

[2] *Johnson's Wonder Working Providence*, p. 166.

[3] *Quincy's History of Harvard University*, vol. I, pp. 265-78.

appears to have acted in that capacity. He was a
tutor as early as July, 1652.[1] Cotton Mather
speaking of him as filling this office says: " With
a rare Faithfulness did he adorn the Station! He
used all the means imaginable to make his Pupils
not only good Scholars, but also good Christians;
and instil into them those things which might render
them rich Blessings unto the Churches of God. Unto
his Watchful and Painful Essays, to keep them close
unto their Academical Exercises, he added Serious
Admonitions unto them about their Interior State,
and (as I find in his Reserved Papers) he Employ'd
his Prayers and Tears to God for them; and had such
a flaming zeal to make them worthy men, that, upon
Reflection, he was afraid, Lest his cares for their
Good, and his affection to them, should so drink up
his very Spirit, as to steal away his Heart from God."[2]

Rev. Increase Mather says that he was "a blessing
as a Tutor in the Colledge. It was an honour to

---

[1] Rev. Increase Mather's dedication to his son's Funeral Sermon
on Wigglesworth, quoted below, is dated July 11, 1705. In it, he
says he was a scholar to Mr. Wigglesworth at college, " above
three and fifty years since."

[2] *Funeral Sermon on Wigglesworth*, page 23.

Corderius that the great Calvin had been his Scholar, and to Mr. Parkhurst that the Learned Juel had been under his Instruction and Tuition, who afterwards took great delight to behold the Sparkling of that Diamond, which himself had first pointed, as one expresseth it. Thus some who were once the Pupils of this worthy man have proved Eminent in these Churches. It will not at all add greatness or respect to his Name for *Me* to say, That I was his Scholar at my first Admission into the Colledge, above three and fifty years since; but I have on that account reason to honour his Memory."[1] The names of the pupils of Mr. Wigglesworth who became eminent.in the churches, are given by Mr. Mather in the margin, namely, Eleazer Mather, John Eliot, Shubael Dummer and Samuel Torry.

One of his common-place books contains two orations, as he calls them, upon eloquence, which were written in 1653, while he held the office of tutor, the last having been finished August 30th, of that year. They appear to have been delivered at

---

[1] Dedication to the preceding *Funeral Sermon*.

the college. I will make a brief extract from each.
The first is entitled *The Prayse of True Eloquence*,
and the second *Concerning True Eloquence and how to
attain it.*

"Eminent," says he, in the first oration, "is the
example of the two best orators that fame has
brought to our ears. Of Cicero, who when he had
naturally a shrill, screaming, ill-tuned voyce rising
to such a note that it indangered his very life, yet
by art and industry he acquired such a commendable
habit, as none with ease could speak more sweetly
than he. And Demosthenes, though he were naturally of a stammering tongue, crasy-body'd and
broken-winded, and withall had accustomed himself
to a jetting uncomely deportment of his body, or
some part of it at least; when to conclude he had
scarce any part of an orator, save only an ardent
desire to be an orator, yet by his indefatigable pains
he so overcame these naturall defects as that he
came to be reputed prince of the Grecian Eloquence.
Though this was not gotten without some further
difficulty and seeming vain attempts. Insomuch
as he was several times quite discouraged, and once

threw all aside, despairing ever to become an orator, because the people laught at his orations. Yet notwithstanding being heartned to it again by some of his wel-willers, he never left striving till he won the prize.

"Go too therefore my fellow-students (for to you I address my speech, my superiors I attempt not to speak to, desiring rather to learn of them more of this nature, but) to you give me leav to say: Let no man hereafter tel me I despair of excelling in this oratoricall faculty, therefore 'tis bootless to endeavor. Who more unlike to make an orator than Demosthenes, except it were one who had no tongue in his head? Yet Demosthenes became *orator optimus.* Tell me not I have made trial once and again, but find my labor fruitless. Thou art not the first that hast made an onset, and bin repelled, neither canst thou presage what renewed endeavors may produce. Would you then obtain this skill? Take Demosthenes his course; gird up your loines, put to your shoulders, and to it again, and again, and agen; let nothing discourage you. Know that to be a dunce, to be a stammerer, unable to bring forth three or four sentences hanging well together, this is an easy matter; but to become an able speaker, *hic labor, hoc opus est.* Would you haue your orations pleas, such as need not be laught at? Why follow him in that also. Let them be such as smell of the lamp, as was said of his; not slovenly I mean, but elaborate, *diurnâ industriâ et nocturnis lucubrationibus elaboratæ,* such as savor of some paines taken with them. A good oration is not made at the first thought, nor scarce at the first writing over. Nor is true eloquence wont to hurry it out thick and threefould, as if each word were running for a wager; nor yet to mutter or whisper it out of a book, after a dreaming manner, with such a voyce as the orator can scarcely heare himself speak; but to utter it with lively affection and to pronounce it distinctly with audible voyce."

The second oration closes as follows: " Gird we up our loins then, and pluck up our spirits that we may tread in the steps of such as haue gone before us; those that have been famous as for other endowments, so for their skill to speak wel, let us follow after them as far as we can, though at a great dis-

tance. Away then with slouth and negligence, we
have examples to quicken us. Away with despond-
ency, we haue examples to incourage us; object
not difficulty, difficultys may be mastered; the
fragrant rose grows upon a thorny bush; the
sweetest nuts have a shel to break before you come
at the kernal, *Difficilia pulchra.* Say not I want a
good invention or voice, 'tis in vain to strive; nay
the more need of study and practise. Art perfects
nature where 'tis defective; nothing is so bad but
it may by endeavors be bettered. Despise not Eloquence, thinking it is better to be skilled in things
then words. Believ it an orator must understand
not onely words but things. An orator is a man of
universal knowledge, or his practise wil quickly
make him so. Say not other things are more need-
ful; what study more necessary than that which
perfects or may perfect a man in all manner of
knowledge. Sound judgment or sapience is the
principal endowment that the mind can reach, and
I know no one exercise that contributes so much
toward it as the practise of declaiming may. Reason
is here put upon its highest and most extensive

improvement. Say not then this skill may be got
hereafter. Noe, the rationall parts as well as the
bodily members are yet in a way of growth; they
may be strengthened if they be exercised; and time
is now given for this purpose; therefore this is the
fittest season; and opportunity waits no man's
leisure. Time and tide will not stay for the king.
There's no redeeming opportunity after it be once
lost. And 'tis the part of a Fool to cry only had I
wist, when 'tis too late.   Finaly run not away with
a piece of Eloquence instead of the whole.   Delight
not in Gingling words without weight; rest not in
weight of Reason alone without Rhetoric.   Sleight
neither; content not yourselves to think wel or
write wel, without ability to utter sutably what you
think or write.

   "These things I have made bold upon several occa-
sions to speak in the behalf of Eloquence; observing
that of later times the study thereof hath been much
neglected amongst us, and the practise of declaiming sundry wayes corrupted; not by all, for there
are some whose good ability's and laudable endeavors in this kind I highly esteem and heartily

embrace; but I wish I might not say by most in some degree or other. The end of all that I haue uttered in this point hitherto is this, to stir up our languishing affections to the right pursuit of true Eloquence, which it may be I should rather have endeavored in another Dialect, had I not feared that some of my auditors are so *exime docti* that they can understand English better than Latin; not so much for any depth of what I had to say, as by reason of your owne deep apprehensions and acquired readiness in that tongue wherein to their no small praise they willingly take pains daly to converse. O difficult task! and yet how readily is it undergone? I say not this to discourage or causelessly to griev any one; but rather to incourage, at least to excite myself and every one to those laudable exercises that have been to our great loss neglected. Let us therefore look about us in time, and quit ourselues for hereafter as becometh an Academy, and not disgrace the name we bear; let us not frustrate the expectations conceived of us. *Oratores! Aratores* rather might some of us be taken for, *non Rostris sed Rastris affluenti.* Let us chase away such cause of

Ignominy for time to come. Let us improve that
priviledge which we alone haue been betrusted with
these many yeares, which tabernacleth amongst us,
but may take her flight we know not how soon.
Finally (my courteous Auditors) and with this word
I shall end. Consider that not so much I press to
these things, as your owne wel-fare; which if they
be duely attended the profit and credit and comfort
wil be your owne." [1]

While he was a tutor, he prepared himself for the
ministry, and before his father's death had preached
several times. [2]   In one of his common-place books [3]
is a sermon, partly in short and partly in long-hand,
from Psalm 81, verse 12, which is headed; "The
2^d Sermon w^h was p^{r}ched by myself at Martin's
Vinyrd, May 1653." Whether this was the second
sermon which he preached or only the second at
Martha's Vineyard, I have no means of ascertaining.

His father, Edward Wigglesworth, whose sickness has before been noticed, lived after that visita-

---

[1] *Common-place Book.*

[2] *Autobiography.*

[3] In the library of the *New England Historic Genealogical Society.*

tion as the son states, "under great and sore affliction
for the space of thirteen years, a pattern of faith,
patience and heavenly-mindedness. Having done
his work in my education and received an answer
to his prayers, God took him to his heavenly rest
where he is now reaping the reward of his labors."[1]
His death occurred at New Haven, October 1, 1653.[2]

---

[1] *Autobiography.*

[2] The grave at New Haven, which has long been pointed out as
that of Col. Edward Whalley, a member of the High Court of
Justice which condemned Charles I to execution, is now generally
admitted to be that of Edward Wigglesworth. The head and foot
stones both bear the initials, " E. W.," and a date. It is supposed
that the date was originally, 1653, the year of Wigglesworth's
death, and that the last figure has since been altered to 8, while
an attempt has been made to alter the third figure to 7. The
figures 5 and 7 both show on the stone; but it is difficult to determine from its appearance which was cut first. A drawing of these
stones and their inscriptions is given in Stiles's *History of the
Judges,* p. 136, and in Barber's *Connecticut Historical Collections,*
p. 154.

The dates of two gravestones in Copp's Hill Burial Ground,
Boston, namely that of Grace Berry who died May 17, 1695, and
that of Joanna, daughter of William and Anne Copp, who died
March 20, 1695–6, have been altered in a similar manner to 1625
and 1625–6 (See Bridgeman's *Epitaphs from Copp's Hill Burial
Ground,* pp. 1 and 4). This alteration makes it appear as though
there were burials in Boston before Gov. Winthrop and his company
removed there. I am told that a gentleman of Boston, who died

He left a widow, Esther, and two children, namely,
Michael, and a daughter about thirteen years old
named Abigail, whom Mr. Wyman, of Charlestown,
supposes to be Abigail successively wife of Benjamin
Sweetser, of Charlestown, and Rev. Ellis Callender
of Boston.[1]

It is not likely that the sermon which he preached
at Martha's Vineyard was preached by him as a
candidate for settlement; for Rev. Thomas Mayhew
had then been the minister there for some years.
" In 1653, the date of the visit of Rev. Mr. Wigglesworth to Martha's Vineyard," writes Mr. Pease of
Edgartown, " the population was so small as not to
require the services of an associate pastor to aid
Mr. Mayhew, then a young man of thirty-three.
Is it not likely that Mr. Wigglesworth was only a
brief visitor on the island : possibly being interested
in the work among the natives, upon which, as you
are aware, Thomas Mayhew entered in advance of
Eliot ? "[2]

---

there in 1865, at the advanced age of 80, stated some years before
his death that he made the alterations when he was a boy.

[1] *N. E. Hist. and Gen. Register*, vol. XVIII, p. 290.

[2] Manuscript letter of Richard L. Pease, Esq., Aug. 21, 1868.

The first call which Mr. Wigglesworth is known
to have received, was from the town of Malden.
The time when it was extended to him, as near as
I can determine, was during the summer or early
in the autumn of 1654.   His predecessor, Rev.
Marmaduke Matthews, whose settlement by the
town had offended the colonial authorities, had been
forced by them to resign his pastoral office, and had
left Malden, probably in 1652.[1] After Mr. Matthews
finished his ministry there, Rev. Nathaniel Upham
seems to have preached a short time as stated
supply.[2] Mr. Wigglesworth was the next settled
minister after Mr. Matthews.   Rev. Mr. Dunster,
president of Harvard College, had a sister Rose,
who was the wife of Joseph Hills, a prominent citizen

[1] *Bi-Centennial Book of Malden*, p. 142.   Rev. Mr. Matthews
preached afterwards at Lynn and other places, and finally returned
to Europe, where he became vicar of his native parish of Swansea
in South Wales.   This living he retained till 1662, when he was
ejected under the Bartholomew Act.   He lived to a good old age
and died about the year 1683.   See Palmer's *Nonconformists's
Memorial* (ed. 1777), vol. I, pp. 627–8.

[2] *American Quarterly Register*, vol. XI, p. 191 ; *Genealogy of the
Upham Family*, p. 11.

of Malden; [1] and Rev. Dr. McClure suggests that it may have been " by means of this connection that Mr. Wigglesworth was here settled in the pastoral office." [2] This is not improbable; though it is stated that students from Harvard College had supplied the pulpit at Malden even before the settlement of Rev. Mr. Matthews. [3] " When about twenty-two years of age," says McClure, probably quoting some memorandum of Wigglesworth himself, [4] " he was invited to preach at Malden. It was some five months before he concluded to accept this invitation. He supplied the pulpit a year and a half, being much troubled to decide what his duty might be, before he was fully inducted into the pastoral office." [5] The precise date

---

[1] *The Malden Messenger*, a newspaper published at Malden, Mass., for April 11, 18 and 25, and May 2 and 16, contains a series of articles by D. P. Corey, Esq., upon the biography of Joseph Hills. For an account of the services of Mr. Hills upon the Laws of Massachusetts Colony, see an article by George H. Moore, Esq., in the *Historical Magazine*, vol. XIII, pp. 85–91.

[2] *Bi-Centennial Book of Malden*, p. 146.

[3] *Wonder Working Providence*, p. 211.

[4] See the *Historical Magazine*, vol. VII, p. 362.

[5] *Bi-Centennial Book of Malden*, pp. 146–7.

of his ordination is not known, but it was probably not far from August 25th, 1656, when he received a letter of dismission from the church at Cambridge. Cotton Mather, in his *Ratio Disciplinæ*, speaking of the election and ordination of ministers, says: "There is a seasonable care taken that, if the candidate were a member of some other church, he have his dismission (his relation declared to be transferred); that, as near as may be, according to the primitive direction, they may choose from among themselves." [1] I presume, therefore, that his ordination did not take place till after Aug. 25th, 1656. The letter of dismission was as follows:

"To the Church of Christ at Malden, Grace and Peace from God our father, and from y⁰ Lord Jesus Christ.

"Whereas, the good hand of Divine Providence hath so disposed that our beloved and highly esteemed brother, Mr. Wigglesworth, hath his residence and is employed in the good work of y⁰ Lord amongst you, and hath seen cause to desire of us Letters Dismissive to your Church, in order to his

---

[1] Mather's *Ratio Disciplinæ* (1726), p. 22.

joining as a member with you. We, therefore, of the Church of Christ at Cambridge, have consented to his Desires herein, and if you shall accordingly proceed to receive him, we do hereby resigne and dismiss him to your holy fellowship, withall certifying that as he was formerly admitted among us with much approbation, so during his abode with us, his conversation was such as did become the gospell, not doubting but that through the grace of Christ, it hath been and will be no otherwise amongst you; and that he will be enabled to approve himself to you in y⁰ Lord as becometh saints.

"Further desiring of the Father of mercies that he may become a chosen and special blessing to you, and you also againe unto him through Christ Jesus.

"We commit him and you all, with ourselves, to him who is our Lord and yours.

"In whom we are,

> "Your loving brethren,
>> Jonathan Mitchell,
>> Richard Champney,
>> Edmund Frost."

"With y* consent of y* brethren of y* Church at Cambridge.

"Cambridge 25 of y* 6th m. 1656." [1]

At that time the ministers in Massachusetts were settled either as *pastors* or *teachers*. The Cambridge Platform, adopted by the Synod of 1648, thus defines the duties of these two kinds of officers: "The Pastor's special work is to attend to exhortation, and therein to administer a word of wisdom; the Teacher is to attend to doctrine and therein to administer a word of knowledge; and either of them to administer the seals of that covenant, unto the dispensation whereof they are called; as also to execute the censures, being but a kind of application of the word; the preaching of which, together with the application thereof, they are alike charged withal." [2]   Their respective duties may perhaps be better understood by the explanation of

---

[1] *Christian Register* (newspaper), June 29, 1850. The signature of Richard Champney is there misprinted Kirkland E. Lamprey.

[2] *Cambridge Platform*, ch. VI, sect. 5. The following texts are cited in support of the position, viz: Eph. IV, 11 ; Rom. XII, 7, 8 ; 1 Cor. XII, 8 ; II Tim. IV, 1, 2 ; Titus, I, 9.

Rev. Dr. McClure: "The pastor," says he, "on whom chiefly devolved the care of the flock when out of the pulpit, was expected to spend his strength mostly in exhortation, persuading and rousing the church to a wise diligence in the Christian calling. The teacher was to indoctrinate the church and labor to increase the amount of Christian knowledge. His workshop was the study; while the pastor toiled in the open field."[1] This distinction had been brought from England; and the different qualifications for the two offices are set forth in detail in *A True Description, out of the Word of God, of the Visible Church*, published in the year 1589.[2]

---

[1] Life of Rev. John Cotton by Rev. A. W. McClure, D.D., p. 115. The difference between a pastor and a teacher is shown more fully in the *Survey of the Summe of Church Discipline*, by Rev. Thomas Hooker (1648), pp. 13–22. See also an article by the late Rev. Samuel Sewall of Burlington, Mass., in the *American Quarterly Register*, Aug., 1840, vol. XIII, p. 37; Trumbull's edition of Lechford's *Plain Dealing*, pp. 17, 18; and the *Congregational Quarterly*, vol. V (1863), pp. 182–3. For an elaborate argument that *pastor* and *teacher*, and also *presbyter* and *bishop* are but names of one office, see Dexter on *Congregationalism* (1868), pp. 77–92.

[2] This is reprinted in Hanbury's *Historical Memorials*, vol. I, pp. 28–34; and in Punchard's *History of Congregationalism* (1841), pp. 364–72.

Where there was only one minister, he was usually ordained as pastor. Mr. Wigglesworth, however, appears to have been ordained as *teacher* of the church at Malden,[1] though his predecessor, Rev. Mr. Matthews, had been *pastor*[2] of that church. It is not probable that it was the intention, in a church of such small means, to support two ministers. Perhaps Mr. Wigglesworth may have thought himself not well fitted for the active duties of parochial life, and may have chosen the office of teacher to indicate the service he was best able to render to his parish. Precedents are not wanting where the only minister of a church was settled as its teacher. This was the case with Rev. John Wilson, the first minister of the first church in Boston. He was chosen and confirmed as teacher

---

[1] In the petition of the inhabitants of Malden to the General Court of Massachusetts, June 7, 1662, he is called teacher, and he is so called also in the title pages of the various editions of the *Day of Doom*.

[2] The deposition of five members of the Malden church, May 16, 1651, quoted in the *Bi-Centennial Book of Malden*, p. 137, calls Mr. Matthews "our reverend pastor."

Aug. 27, 1630,[1] and, ordained as pastor Nov. 22, 1632.[2] Mr. Wigglesworth's first colleague, Rev. Benjamin Bunker, was ordained as pastor;[3] and so probably were his other colleagues, Rev. Messrs. Blackman and Cheever. After the dismission of Rev. Mr. Cheever, in 1686, I presume that Mr. Wigglesworth, who then became the sole minister, took the office and name of pastor, for he is so styled on his gravestone and in the inventory of his estate. However, on the title page of the editions of the *Day of Doom*, printed after he ceased to have a colleague, he still continued to be termed "teacher," and it is possible that he never himself assumed any other name.

"It was not long," says Cotton Mather, "after his coming to *Malden*, that a sickly constitution so prevailed upon him as to confine him from his

---

[1] Savage's *Winthrop*, vol. I, 1st ed. p. 31 ; 2d ed. p. 36.

[2] *Ibid.*, 1st ed. p. 96 ; 2d ed. p. 114.

[3] Rev. Samuel Danforth calls him Pastor, in entries which he made on the records of the First Church in Roxbury, giving the date of Mr. Bunker's ordination and death. So does Mr. Wigglesworth in his elegy.

Publick Work, for some whole sevens of years."
If, as is here asserted, the number of years that he
was unable to officiate regularly in the pulpit was
a multiple of seven, that term of years was probably
twenty-eight.   This would make its beginning
sometime in the year 1657 or 1658; for we know
that his recovery was in 1685 or 1686, since, according to the writer just quoted, Mr. Wigglesworth
actively performed his ministerial duties for about
twenty years before his death;[1] and besides in the
spring of the year last named he spoke of his recent
recovery in his prayer at the Election Sermon
preached by him before the Massachusetts General
Court.   If twenty-one years was intended by Mather,
the beginning of his confinement from public work
would be 1664 or 1665, that is, not long after his
return from Bermuda.

His health had begun to fail while he was a tutor
at college. Cotton Mather preserves a memorandum
by him, June 20, 1652, in which his bodily weakness
is mentioned;[2] and in some lines prefixed to the

---

[1] *Funeral Sermon,* p. 24.

[2] *Ibid.,* p. 40.

Day of Doom, his "sufferings of more than ten years length," are alluded to, which would carry the time back to about the same date. Some of the principal inhabitants of Malden in a petition to the General Court written June 7, 1662, say: " Our teacher, Mr. Wigglesworth, also hath been *long* visited with verie great weaknesses from which it is feared he will not be recovered." [1] He seems to have had a fit of sickness soon after he received a call from the Malden church, for Mather quotes some reflections of his " after he was invited unto Malden, and then was taken off by Long Sickness." [2] His private memoranda, between March 14, 1658, and April 4, 1662, contain frequent references to his ill health.

By the summer of 1659, his health had become so impaired that he had serious thoughts of resigning his ministerial office; for a memorandum by him, dated July 30th, of that year, mentions that he had thoughts of visiting Rowley and consulting his relatives and friends there as to laying down his

---

[1] *Bi-Centennial Book of Malden,* p. 59.

[2] *Funeral Sermon,* p. 40.

office.[1] Sometime after, but without date, he records
the following reflections in his common-place book :

"Reasons that move me at this time earnestly to
desire deliverance from this long continued and
increasing weakness, are such as these :

"1. The great affliction that it is to my soul
many wayes. As first, I am detained from the
libertys of God's house and ordinances for the most
part, and when I can go forth my weakness of body
much hindreth intention of mind and consequently
my profiting.

"2. It hindreth from the benefit of Christian
conference, counsel, &c. I cannot go abroad to
meet with friends, nor am I wel able to discourse

---

[1] His brother-in-law, William Hobson of Rowley, died in July,
1659, and was buried the 17th of that month. (*Collections of the
Essex Institute*, V, 162). About a fortnight after this burial, Mr.
Wigglesworth made the memorandum above referred to, which is
as follows : "*July* 30, 1659. 1 h. thoughts of a jo'ney to Rowley.
My ends are these : 1. To cōfort my distressed friends. 2. To
advize about my ōw health & laying dōw my work. 3. To advize
and help about ordering yᵉ goods, to receiv oʳ p't & pʳvēt my
fathers frō scattering by p'cels. 4. To right oʳ accoūts about
monys *lent & sent* frō me by Bro : Hobson." Instead of the words
in italics, the word "rec'd" was first written and erased.

an hour with any that come to me. My distemper
will not suffer me to be in any one place or posture
half an hour at a time.

"3. It is a sore hindrance to my personal com-
munion with God and holy walking. I cannot
take that pains with my carnal heart that its neces-
sitys require cannot make a fervent prayer but my
strength fayleth before I have half unburthened
my heart or spread my case before the lord. I
cannot think a few serious thoughts, scarce once in
a whole day many times, except it be now and then
a short ejaculation, which doth not so effectually
take off the heart from things below and carry it
into heaven as set and solemn meditation was wont
to do.

"4. I have not nor can have the benefit of a particular calling which should keep out evil thoughts
and temptations. Hence my mind and heart are
overrun with vain and sometimes with vile imagina-
tions and affections, even as the husbandman's field
is overgrown with weeds when he hath not strength
to til. This is sorest exercise and the very sting of
myne affliction, that corruption gets such great

advantage through my bodily weaknes. This makes
life a burden, becaus my dayes are spent in vanity,
and my vanity not onely brings vexation with itself
but breeds distances between God and my soul,
and it hath not been with me of late as in times
past either in respect of peace and comfort or of
suppleness of frame. Onely the Lord hath given
a little reviving of late before the last Lord's
supper and since this last week, and I do earnestly
desire that I might lose myself and my frame no
more, but be stil more recovered out of the hand
of my corruptions and live better at last than at
first." [1]

This was written in 1660 or 1661. Later —
probably in December, 1661 — he enters the following in his common-place book or diary: "The
Brethren are now below considering and consulting
about a future supply and a constant help in the
ministry; as also whether I am call'd to lay down
my place or not. Father, I leave my self and all
my concernments with thee. I have neither way

---

[1] *Common-place Book.*

of subsistence nor house to put my head in if turn'd
out here.   But Lord I desire to be at thy disposing.
Let thy fatherly care appear towards me in these
my straits, as hitherto it hath done, O my God; for
other friend or helper beside thee I have none,
Lord I beleev; help my unbelief." [1]

I have not been able to determine what the disease was with which Mr. Wigglesworth was so long
afflicted, and from which, at length, he was so far
relieved as to spend about twenty of the last years
of his life in comparative health.   In the fall of
1868, I collected together the various notices of his
disease and his feelings which I found in his manuscripts and elsewhere, and submitted them to my
friend Samuel Abbott Green, M.D., of Boston, in
the hope that he might be able to form some conjecture as to the nature of this sickness.   But the
data furnished him were not sufficient for him to
form an opinion.   In returning my memoranda,
Sept. 12, 1868, he wrote me: "I am sorry that I
cannot make out a *diagnosis* as physicians call it.

---

[1] *Common-place Book.*

I have shown your case to several, all of whom
agree that the data are not sufficient to warrant an
accurate conclusion." I also submitted them to
Ebenezer Alden, M.D., of Randolph, with no better
result. Rev. Dr. McClure speaks of his disease as
" a pulmonary complaint, perhaps the asthma,"[1]
Dr. Alden thinks it evident that he had the asthma ;
but says, that the asthma will not account for all
his symptoms.

His first wife was Mary, daughter of Humphrey
Reyner, of Rowley. She was a niece of Rev. John
Reyner, who was settled successively at Plymouth
and Dover as the minister to those churches. It is
not unlikely that when they were children, Mr.
Wigglesworth and his wife were fellow passengers
from England. The precise date of their marriage
is not known, but it was probably not far from the
time when he received his call to the ministry at
Malden. Their married life was of short duration,
Mrs. Wigglesworth died on the twenty-first day of
December, 1659, at about two o'clock in the

---

[1] *Bi-Centennial Book of Malden*, p. 153.

morning.[1] She left one child only, a daughter less
than four years old. Her husband felt the blow
keenly. His feelings on the occasion are thus recorded: "Oh it is a heart-cutting and astonishing
stroke in itself. Lord help me to bear it patiently
and to profit by it. Help me to honor thee now in
the fiers, by maintaining good thoughts of thee,
and speaking good and submissive words concerning thee. And, oh, teach me to dy every day. Fit
me for that sweet society she is gone unto, where
solitarines shal no more affright or afflict me. Oh,
Lord, make up in thyself what is gone in the creature. I believe thou canst and wilt do it; but oh
help my unbelief."

As far as I can ascertain, Mr. Wigglesworth lived
a widower for about twenty years after the death of
his first wife, at which time the wife whom I suppose
to be his second was not born.

Though the feebleness of his health prevented
him from officiating regularly, if at all, in the pulpit,

<hr/>

[1] The year is not given in the memorandum in his *Common-place Book*, from which I obtain the month, day and hour, but there is little doubt that it was 1659. Possibly it may have been 1660. It was after July, 1659.

he did not permit his time to pass away in idleness. Literary labor was made to supply the place of the duties to which he had devoted his life, but which he found himself unable to perform. The tongue was forced to be mute in exhorting and instructing his fellow-men, but the pen could be used for that purpose; and he decided to call it to his aid. Remembering that,

> " A verse may find him who a sermon flies,
> And turn delight into a sacrifice," [1]

he sought, with the attractions of rhyme,

> " To set forth truth and win men's souls to bliss." [2]

The *Day of Doom*, his first poetical production of which we have any intimation, was commenced as early as January, 1661–2. On the 29th of that month, he made this entry in his *Common-place Book:* " I desire with all my heart and might to serve my Lord Christ (who is my best and onely friend and supporter) in finishing this work which

---

[1] Herbert. *The Church Porch.*

[2] J. Mitchell. On the *Day of Doom* and its author.

I am preparing for the press, acknowledging that the Lord hath dealt abundantly better with me then I deserve, if he shall please to accept such a poor piece of service at my hands, and give me leisure to finish it. I delight in his service and glory, and the good of poor souls, though my endeavors this way should rather occasion loss then outward advantage to my self. Lord let me find grace in thy sight. And who can tell but this work may be my last; for the world seem now to account me a burden (I mean divers of our chief ones) whatever their words pretend to the contrary. Lord, be thou my habitation and hiding place, for other I have none. Do thou stand my friend when all other friends fail me, as they are now like to do. I will not torment myself with feares concerning the future, for I know thou art alsufficient and canst either provide for me in my weakness or recover me out of my weakness by a word after all means used to no purpose, or els thou canst make me welcome in Heaven when the world is weary of me. Lord undertake for me, for mine eys are unto thee. *Tibi Domine, &c.*"

9

On the next page he writes: "It pleased the Lord to carry me through the difficulty of the fore-mentioned work, both in respect of bodily strength and estate, and to give vent for my books, and greater acceptance then I could have expected, so that of 1800 there were scarce any unsold (or but few) at the yeers end; so that I was a gainer by them and not a loser. Moreover I have since heard of some success of those my poor labours. For all which mercies, I am bound to bless the Lord. Who am I &c.? About 4 yeers after they were reprinted with my consent, and I gave them the proofs and Marginal notes to affix."

The *Day of Doom* must have been completed and published some time in the year 1662, and pro-bably in the summer or spring of that year; for the voyage to Bermuda, which will be subsequently noticed, and on which he sailed the 23d of Septem-ber, 1663, was, according to his own statement, made after the first impression of his book was sold, which seems to have taken about a year. The fact that less than forty-two years after the Landing of the Pilgrims, an edition consisting of eighteen hundred copies of a volume of poetry was sold in New England in a year's time is most wonderful. Considering the small number of our population at that time, and its sparseness, this indicates a popularity almost, if not quite equal, to that of *Uncle Tom's Cabin* in our own day.

At least ten editions of the *Day of Doom* have appeared, two of them in England.[1] In noticing the last edition edited by William H. Burr, and published in 1867 at New York city, Evert A. Duyckinck, Esq., the senior author of the *Cyclopœdia of American Literature*, thus writes :

"The reprint of this quaint old poem of the early Puritan era in New England, crosses like a dark thread the gaily colored literature of the day. It is indeed a grim utterance of the past when theology, like other medicines administered to a sinful generation, was anything but sugar-coated. There is probably not at this day — Doctor Holmes's Bellamy Stoker to the contrary notwithstanding — a preacher in New England who would go to work with his flock in so cool, merciless a way to ' shut

---

[1] For the different editions of this poem, see *Appendix* No. II.

the gates of mercy on mankind' as the Reverend
Michael Wigglesworth, 'Teacher of the Church at
Malden,' Massachusetts, in the seventeenth century.
Justice with the terrors of her law, fearfully over-
shadows Mercy in his poem, which, in spite of
occasional halting, is really a meritorious composition in its way, written in good vigorous English
and sounding rhythm.   There are a great many
home truths in it, too, which the men of every age
would do well to profit by; but it is impossible
after reading his verses to resist the impression that
the writer took a positive delight in picturing the
remediless fate of the lost.   It is not enough that
he exhibits the awful separation of the just and the
unjust at the final day, but the former must be
represented with a deity of ineffable love adding to
the miseries of the condemned." [1]

The anonymous author [2] of the biographical
sketch prefixed to the Newburyport edition printed

----

[1] *Historical Magazine* (New York, 1868), 2d series, vol. III, p. 127.
[2] Miss Mary T. Little of Newbury, a descendant of Wigglesworth, after reading an extract from the sketch in the *Newburyport
Herald*, wrote me that the style reminded her of Rev. John Snell-

in 1811, gives this opinion of the *Day of Doom:*
"It breathes throughout a strain of piety. The
answers of Christ to the pleas of those who appear
before his tribunal, are always pertinent, ingenious,
just, and frequently not unworthy of the exalted
character of the judge. True, there are some things
in this composition which do not perfectly suit the
moderate religion of the present day; yet whether
this be owing to the improvement or degeneracy of
our virtue, I leave to be answered by the lives and
consciences of my brethren."

Another poem, though much shorter, was written,
in the year 1662, by Mr. Wigglesworth. The
manuscript of this poem was seen by Rev. Dr.
McClure when he compiled the memoir in the *Bi-
Centennial Book of Malden.* I have not been able to
learn whether it is now in existence or not.
McClure gives the following description of it:

"Among his unpublished writings, we find a poem
bearing the title: 'God's Controversy with New

___

ing Popkin, D.D., who was in 1811 the pastor of a church in Newburyport, and whose church, she thought, Mr. Little, the senior
publisher, attended.

England,' written in the time of the great drought
Anno 1662.   By a lover of New England's pro-
sperity."   This was a dark time for the Puritans on
either side of the Atlantic.   It was the year of the
passage of the infamous " Act of Uniformity."
The house of Stuart, then but newly restored to the
British throne, was breathing out threatenings and
slaughter against the nonconformists.   The colonial
charters and liberties of New England were placed
in the utmost peril; and our fathers were quaking
under the apprehension of losing all that they had
sought and found on these desolate shores.   It is
not strange, that they should be disposed, at such
a gloomy season, to look upon the sickness and
drought, with which they were then afflicted, as so
many direct tokens of divine displeasure at some
degeneracy among themselves.

" In the poem before us, Mr. Wigglesworth, after
a brief ' Request to the Reader,' couched both in
English and Latin verse, goes on to describe ' New
England planted, prospered, declining, threatened,
punished.'   He gives at first, an interesting sketch
of the earliest and best days, the golden age of

New England. Next he speaks in a few lines, of
the degeneracy of the times in which he wrote.
Then the Divine Being is introduced, in a different
and more elegiac strain, uttering rebukes and de-
nouncing retribution, unless there shall be a speedy
repentance. The poet closes with a sketch of the
recent divine judgments upon the people, with a
blast of the woe-trumpet announcing direr calami-
ties at hand, and with a fervent protestation of his
love and attachment to the land of his adoption." [1]

Cotton Mather notices "a short voyage unto another country for the recovery of his health," which
he took after his ministry was interrupted by sickness; and he, himself, gives details of it as follows:
"After the first impression of my books was sold,
I had a great mind to go to Bermuda, and found
many incouragers and incouragements thereto.
Providence made way for it wonderfully, by providing John Younglove [2] to go with me, and by

---

[1] *Bi-Centennial Book of Malden,* p. 149.

[2] Perhaps the Rev. John Younglove, afterwards of Brookfield,
Mass., Hadley, Mass., and Suffield, Ct. He died at Suffield June 3,
1690. See Boltwood's *Hadley Genealogies* appended to Judd's
History of Hadley, Mass., p. 605.

sending over Mr. Barr from thence, who both informed of the place, incouraged me by the healthfulness of it, moderate and temperate weather, cheapness of diet, &c. And also, he having a vessel for his return, accommodated me. The Lord also ordered it so that I got a pretty competent estate to take with me. Physicians encouraged me (except Mr. Winthrope whose counsel came too late, nor did his reasons seem sufficient); so we set sayl about the 23 of September, 1663. Our voyage was long, and the latter part of it very tedious, by stormy weather and cross winds, so that it was a full month ere we got thither; by which long and tedious voyage no doubt but I received much hurt, and got so much cold as took away much of the benefit of that sweet and temperate air; and so hindered my recovery, and lost me much of that little time that I stayed there. Yet I did accustom myself by degrees to the air, more then I could here, or can do to this day: the calmness and gentle warmth of the winter there giving me much advantage that way which I want here in New England. After I had continued at Bermuda about seven months and

a half, finding the alteration on my body not great,
and withall a general faint cold that few escaped,
making me very unable to bear the heat of the
month of May.   I was doubtful that the heat of
summer might prove as disadvantagious to me as
the mildness of winter was like to be profitable;
also their diet was so faint that I feared it would
not sute me in any measure, especially in the ex-
tremity of heat (at which time of the yeer it was
like to be the meanest); also my flower, whereof I
had eight barrels with me, not selling for any price
nor being of any use to me almost, becaus they
could not make a loaf of good bread with it, John
Younglove also being unwilling to stay above a
yeer with me, I began to think it better to return
home, then to let slip that opportunity which God
sent by a vessel of Mr. Willoughbies.   I found also
the charges greater then my expectation or information, &c., and I found their housing very mean
and unfit to keep out either cold or heat.   These
things were the grounds of my so speedy return;
which by the good hand of God upon us was a
short and comfortable return, the Lord sending us

10

moderate weather, and bringing us into Charls-river
in twelve days. In this our voyage homeward, I
was so afflicted with costiveness that in eight dayes,
I could not attain a stool, which made me eat very
sparingly; yet the God of my life and of all my
deliverances brought me out of this trouble, and
brought me home in some competent measure of
Health, blessed be his name. Yet I was sorely exercised in my mind, and much puzzled to know
what to make of the Lords dealings with me, who
seemed to incourage me so many wayes to the
voyage beforehand, and yet crossed me and disap-
pointed me in sundry respects and made that under-
taking fruitless, and not given me incouragement
to tarry there upon the Triall. Peradventure I was
too impetuous in desiring of Health. I have cause
to suspect my own heart in this case. Perhaps I
was too bigg with expectation of somewhat from
the creature that is not in the creature. I find my
heart very subject to this Vanity, just as a sick man
conceits another room or another bed would ease
him, if not cure him; so I have been too apt to
conceit another place or condition or posture would

cure me (or to look too much to the creature) and this vanity must be corrected with such costly experiments as was this voyage to Bermuda. Again, peradventure the Lord removed me for a season, that he might set a better watchman over this his flock, and a more painful labourer in his vineyard. This was one thing that I aimed at in removing (to help the people's modesty in this case) and I do beleeve that the Lord aimed at it in removing me for a season.

"Finally it may be the Lord carried me to Bermuda for a Time that he might make me more welcome here to his people at my return. And indeed I have found more love from the people generally (both Church and Town) since my return then I did before and they have done more for me of their own accord when left to their liberty then they had done for some yeers before I went away. And the Lord hath also made me more serviceable to them, at least in a private way, and given more incouragement and success in the conversion of souls then ever before. What shall I render to the Lord for all his benefits? How mysterious are his dealings. He brings meat out of the Eater. O blessed be thy gracious name, most dear Father."

Some remarks upon his sickness, follow in the common-place book from which the foregoing is extracted. "My bodily weaknesses" he writes, " evidently increase and grow upon me ; especially that old Malady that annoys me most by night. And what fear and distress it often (yea, ever and anon) puts me into, Lord thou knowest ; for my sighs and groanings (with my tears) are not hid from thee. By thine immediate hand it hath hitherto been quelled and restrained, when all the means that I can think off are of no force. But still it continueth and my bondage is greatly increased by reason of it, having no means nor medicine that yield's any releef. Mr. Alcock[1] is gone whose Plaister was heretofore of great efficacy for the repressing of it when more troublesome then ordinary. Mr. Winthrope being consulted, dares not meddle at such a distance. I have spent much

---

[1] Probably John Alcock, a nephew of Rev. Thomas Hooker, who was graduated at H. C., in 1646, and practiced physic in Hartford, Ct. He died March 29, 1667, aged about 40.

time and Labor myself in studying and seeking
after what might be helpful, but yet I find no releefe
in anything, but am forced to look immediately to
the Lord for help and blessed be his name he hath
many and many a time wonderfully and graciously
answered me and rebuked it for me.

"After much exercise this way and many secret
sighs unto the Lord under the pressure of this and
many other infirmities, the Providence of the Lord
hath presented to me and provided for me an unexpected and unknown medicine, a box of Mr.
Lockier's Pills (whose booke with some pills my
cosen Reyner met with at his Landlords at Mend-
ham and signifying to me the high commendations
given them by their author and the experience of
sundry there of good by them, at my request he
procured me a sight of the book and a box of
the pills for 5s.). And these pills I am now
beginning to take this 19th of March, 1669,
Lord be pleased even beyond expectation to bless
them, as thou hast by an unexpected and strange
Providence presented them to me and provided
them for me.

"1. I have learnt by long experience that the best of means can do me no good without thee.

"2. I beleeve that Jehovah the Creator of the ends of the earth can do all things. Nothing is too hard for thee, therefore thou canst cure me yet, that have been so long incurable.

"3. Thou art all-gracious; therefore I beleeve there is goodnes enough in thee to move thee to do such a great work for a most unworthy sinner; enough in Jesus Christ though no goodness in me to move thee.

"4. I owne my utter unworthiness and vileness, and therefore justify thee if thou never do it for me.

"5. I therefore begg humble submission to thy soveraigne and holy will in the event, that I may not repine nor be discontented though things go cross to my desire. Help me to put my mouth in the dust and to say not my will but the Lord's will be done. All our work is duty; issues belong to God.

"6. Nevertheless, if for thine owne Name's sake it may please thee to Grant my suit; Man's ex-

tremity is God's opportunity, and makes for the
advancement of God's power and grace, oh, therefore be seen in the Mount."

The winter after Mr. Wigglesworth sailed on his
voyage in search of health, an associate minister,
Rev. Benjamin Bunker, was settled over the church
at Malden. He was ordained December 9, 1663,
as "pastor" according to Rev. Samuel Danforth's
entry on the Roxbury Church Records. Mr. Bunker was a son of George Bunker of Charlestown,
where he was born in the year 1635. His father
owned land in Charlestown on a hill, which has
taken its name from him, and which has become
famous for the battle fought near it June 17, 1775.
Benjamin, who was then twenty-eight years old,
was a graduate of Harvard College in the class
of 1658. His ministry at Malden lasted more than
six years, and was terminated by death February
3, 1669–70. Mr. Wigglesworth wrote his elegy [1]
in which he gives him a high character for sincerity,

---

[1] An autograph copy of this poem is preserved in the library of
the Historic-Genealogical Society, No. 18 Somerset street, Boston,
Essex manuscripts, vol. I, folio 8.

modesty and devotion to his calling. A character like this must have excited a warm friendship in the breast of Mr. Wigglesworth, rendering their connection most pleasant and fraternal.

About seven years after the publication of *The Day of Doom*, Mr. Wigglesworth completed a new poem. The title which he gave it was, *Meat out of the Eater; or Meditations concerning the Necessity, End and Usefulness of Afflictions unto God's Children; All tending to Prepare them* FOR *and Comfort them* UNDER *the Cross.* "The first title" says Rev. Dr. McClure, "alludes to Samson's riddle; and truly, affliction which had devoured so many of the good man's joys, was made to disgorge far richer treasures than it took away. The second and larger part of the book is entitled, *Riddles Unriddled; or Christian Paradoxes broke open, smelling like sweet spice new taken out of boxes.*

> ' Each Paradox is like a Box
> That Cordials rare encloseth ;
> This Key unlocks, op'neth the Box,
> And what's within discloseth ;
> That whoso will may take his fill,
> And gain where no man loseth.'

"As the first part of the book treats of afflictions in general, so this part dwells upon more particular trials and temptations. The several paradoxes, expounded at length in divers extensive "songs" and " meditations," are comprised in the following lines, which form the *thema* to which he tuned his harp:

> 'Light in Darkness, Sick men's Health,
> Strength in Weakness, Poor men's Wealth,
> In Confinement, Liberty,
> In Solitude, Good Company,
> Joy in Sorrow, Life in Deaths,
> Heavenly Crowns for Thorny Wreaths,
> Are presented to the view,
> In the Poems that ensue,
> If my Trials had been thine,
> These would cheer thee more than Wine.' " [1]

His common-place book contains these references to that work: "Sept. 17, 1669, I have been long imployed in a great work composing Poems about the cross. I have already found exceeding much help and assistance from Heaven, even to admiration, so that in three weeks time, I have transcribed

[1] *Bi-Centennial Book of Malden,* p. 148.

three sheets fair, and made between whiles above 100 staves of verses besides. Some dayes the Lord hath so assisted me that I have made neer or above 20 staves. For which his great mercy I bless his name from my soul, desiring stil to make him my α and ω in this great work. Lord assist me now this day. *Tu mihi principium tu mihi finis eris. à deo et ad deum.* τα παντα.

" 18. Thee Lord I stil desire to serve in this great work; thou hast been with me graciously hitherto this day, for which I bless thy holy name. Oh be with me still; help me to make thee my α and ω for without thee *nihil possum,*   *   *   *

" Lord be present with me this day, Subdue and mortify my sinful passions which are very headstrong; but I hate them and am grieved for them ; O pardon me for Christ's sake ; Assist me to walk with thee, and in particular in this great work of composing and writing out, &c. *Tu mihi principium, tu mihi Finis eris.* Sept. 29. The Lord did assist me much this day, so that I wrote 5 sides fair and made out 11 or 12 staves more though the day was cold and I wrought with some difficulty.

" Sept. 30. Lord assist me this day, for I am thy servant. Amen.

*   *   *   *   *   *

" And now I do seriously and heartily begg help and assistance for I am deeply sensible that without thee I can do nothing, and for thee I desire to do all. Oh guide my head, heart, hand and all, that I may serve thee with all my might this day for Christ's sake and for the honor of thy name. Amen. October 4, 69.

*   *   *   *   *   *

"I am now upon the last Head (Heavenly Crowns, &c.) * * * October, 15.

" *Cum deo et Christo*, October 16. * * * *Sine te nihil possum. Tu mihi α and ω.*

" And now through thy rich grace and daily assistance I have done composing, *Laus deo.* * * * Amen.   October 18.[1] My Birth day and it was the

---

[1] This date looks something like 28 ; but as it follows an entry October 16, and as entries October 19, 20 and 21, follow it, there is little doubt that it was intended for 18. If so, *Meat out of the Eater* was finished Monday morning, October 18, 1669. From this entry we obtain the month and day on which Mr. Wigglesworth was born.

birth day of this book, it being finished (i. e. fully composed) this morning."

It is presumed that this poem was published soon after it was completed, that is, in 1669 or early in 1670. It proved very successful, though not so popular as the author's previous publication. Except, however, the *Day of Doom* and the *Bay Psalm Book*, I know of no poetical volume published in New England previous to the Revolution, that has passed through so many editions as *Meat out of the Eater.*[1]

The second colleague of Mr. Wigglesworth was Rev. Benjamin Blackman. He was a classmate at Harvard College with Mr. Wigglesworth's cousin, by marriage, Rev. John Reyner, Jr., both having graduated there in 1663.[2] The town records state that he " supplied the desk four years and left in the year 1678."[3] He removed to Scarborough, in Maine.[4]

---

[1] A collation of all the editions of this book that I have met with is printed in APPENDIX No. II.

[2] *Catalogus Universitatis Harvardianæ*, ed. 1869, p. 3.

[3] *Bi-Centennial Book of Malden*, p. 157.

[4] For further information respecting Rev. Mr. Blackman, see *Bi-Centennial Book of Malden*, p. 156; *History of Scarboro'* in the

In or about the year 1679, Mr. Wigglesworth married again. He had then, for aught I can find to the contrary, been a widower since the death of his first wife, a period of about twenty years. The Christian name of his wife was Martha, and her surname is supposed to have been Mudge; at least, her husband, in his will, bequeaths to some of her children property which had been left them by their " grandfather Mudge." I presume she was a daughter of Thomas Mudge of Malden.[1] She was then about eighteen years of age, some six years younger than his daughter; and had been his servant maid or perhaps housekeeper. His friend and former pupil, Rev. Increase Mather of Boston, in a letter to him written May 8, 1679, tries to dissuade him from this marriage. Her obscure parentage, her youth, and her being no church member, " nor so much as baptised," are severally objected to.

--- --- ---

Maine Historical Collections, vol. III, p. 155 ; *Savage's Genealogical Dictionary*; and *Hinman's First Puritan Settlers of Connecticut*, 2d ed., art. Blackman.

[1] See *Memorials of the Mudge Family*, by Alfred Mudge (Boston, 1868), pp. 181 and 194.

" To take one," writes he, " that was never baptised into such neerness of relation, seemeth contrary to the Gospell, especially for a minister of Christ to doe it. The like never was in New England. Nay I question whether the like hath been known in the Christian world." [1] It seems that his relatives also did not approve of the marriage.[2] Before this letter was sent, Mr. Mather received by the hand of Rev. Mr. Blackman, who either was still residing at Malden or had recently been there on a visit, a particular statement of the reasons for the marriage; This was submitted by Mr. Mather to Messrs. Eliot, Nowell, Allen and Willard; but these gentlemen, though they do not seem to have been satisfied with his reasons, did not advise him to break off the match.[3]

Notwithstanding the objections to this marriage, it does not appear that Mr. Wigglesworth ever regretted it. On the contrary, in a letter written less than a year after her death, he expresses the

---

[1] *Massachusetts Historical Collections*, vol. XXXVIII, p. 95.

[2] *Ibid.*, p. 94.

[3] *Ibid*, pp. 95, 96.

opinion that, under God, she was a means of his
recovering a better state of health.[1] Their married
life lasted about eleven years, she having died Sept.
4, 1690, aged twenty-eight.[2] She left one son and
five daughters.

His third and last colleague was Rev. Thomas
Cheever, a son of his old New Haven schoolmaster, who had removed to the Massachusetts
colony nearly thirty years before and was then the
Master of the Free School in Boston. Thomas
Cheever was born August 23, 1658,[3] long after Mr.
Wigglesworth had passed from under the father's
instruction; and was graduated at Harvard College
in the class of 1677.[4] At his coming to Malden,
he was in his twenty-second year. He began to
preach there on the fourteenth of February, 1679–80,
but was not ordained till the twenty-seventh of
July, 1681.[5] His connection with this parish lasted

New England Historical and Genealogical Register, vol. XVII,
p. 141. Letter to Mrs. Sybil Avery, March 23, 1690–1.

[2] *Ibid.*, vol. IX, p. 328.

[3] *Savage's New England Genealogical Dictionary*, vol. I, p. 371.

[4] *Catalogus Universitatis Harvardianæ*, ed. 1869, p. 4.

[5] *Bi-Centennial Book of Malden*, p. 157.

about six years, including the time he acted as stated supply. The spring after Mr. Cheever commenced preaching at Malden, Mr. Wigglesworth was made a freeman of Massachusetts, being admitted at the session of the General Court held May 19, 1680.[1]

In 1684, Rev. Increase Mather wrote to Mr. Wigglesworth concerning some employment in the gift of the college authorities that it was proposed to bestow upon him. In the reply to this letter, dated "Malden, Octob. 27, 1684," he declines the offer. " I cannot think," he writes, " my bodily strength competent to undertake or manage such a weighty work as you mention, if it were desired; nor have I reason to judge myself in any measure fit upon other accounts Wherefore I hope the Colledge and Overseers will think of and apply themselves to a fitter person."[2] Dr. Appleton, the compiler of the index to the volume of the *Massachusetts Historical Collections*, where this letter is printed, considers the work tendered to and declined

[1] *Massachusetts Colony Records*, vol. v, p. 539.
[2] *Massachusetts Historical Collections*, vol. XXXVIII, p. 615.

by him, to be the presidency of Harvard College, which seems probable. He also thinks that Mr. Wigglesworth was elected to the office.[1] The college was then without a president, the last person who held the office, Rev. John Rogers, having died on the second of the preceding July. The presidency was vacant till the eleventh of June, 1685, when Rev. Increase Mather, who had before temporarily acted as president, was requested to discharge the duties of the place. During the vacancy the chair is said to have been offered to Rev. Joshua Moody.[2]

Charges brought against Rev. Mr. Cheever, the pastor at Malden, of words spoken by him, caused much strife in the church and parish.[3] Letters were sent out by the church, in March, 1686, for a council to advise in the matter.[4] Rev. Increase Mather was the moderator of this council, which met

---

[1] *Massachusetts Historical Collections*, vol. XXXVIII, p. 735.

[2] Quincy's *History of Harvard University*, vol. I, p. 38 ; Peirce's *History of Harvard University*, pp. 49 and 56.

[3] D. P. Corey, Esq.

[4] *New England Historical and Genealogical Register*, vol. VI, p. 72.

at Malden on the seventh of April,[1] and adjourned to Boston, where meetings were held May 20 and 27, and June 10.[2] The result of the council was unfavorable to Mr. Cheever; but the church was advised to grant him " a loving dismission."[3] Mr. Cheever was dismissed that year,[4] and, lived in retirement nearly thirty years.   On the nineteenth of October, 1715, he was settled as pastor of the First church in Chelsea, where he officiated for over thirty-four years, and where he died on the twenty-seventh of December, 1749, at the advanced age of 91.[5] Two sermons preached at Malden, while he was settled at Chelsea, namely in 1722 and 1725, were printed in 1726.

About this time the health of Mr. Wigglesworth had been in a great measure restored. At the annual election, May 12, 1686, he was brought out from his seclusion to preach the customary sermon before the General Court of the colony. In his

---

[1] *New England Historical and Genealogical Register*, vol. VI, p. 73.

[2] D. P. Corey, Esq. [3] *Ibid.*

[4] *Bi-Centennial Book of Malden*, p. 157.

[5] Savage's *New England Genealogical Dictionary*, vol. I, p. 372.

prayer he expressed a fear that this might be the
last of their days,[1] probably alluding to the uncer-
tainty that then rested upon the fate of the colonial
government. The charter having in 1684 been
declared vacant,[2] the people were daily expecting
a commission for a new government to supercede
the old; and rumors were rife that caused them
great anxiety. Their suspense was soon ended.
Two days after, Friday, May 14, the English frigate
Rose arrived at Boston, bringing a commission
to one of their own people, Joseph Dudley, as
president, and to other gentlemen as members
of the Council of New England.[3] On the 25th

---

[1] Chief Justice Sewall, in his unpublished Diary, notices Mr.
Wigglesworth's preaching the election sermon and adds : " In's
prayer sd, That may know y⁰ things of our peace in y⁰ our day,
and it may be y⁰ last of our days. Acknowledged God as to y⁰
Election and bringing forth him as 'twere a dead Man, had been
reckon'd among y⁰ dead, to preach." *American Quarterly Register*, vol. XI, p. 193.

[2] Hutchinson's *History of Massachusetts*, vol. I ; 1st and 2d ed.,
p. 340 ; 3d ed., p. 306.

[3] *New England Historical and Genealogical Register*, vol. VIII,
p. 20. Hutchinson's *History of Massachusetts*, vol. I, 1st and 2d ed.,
p. 341 ; 3d ed., p. 306, says the 15th.

of the month the President and Council assumed the government at Boston,[1] without opposition from the colonial authorities or from the
people, who however saw with regret their inde-
pendence wrested from them. Not till after the
deposition of Gov. Andros, I presume, was another
Election Sermon preached at Boston.[2]

At this session of the General Court it was
" ordered that Mr. Humphrey Davy and Mr. Treasurer,[3] give the Reuerend Mr. Michael Wigglesworth
the thanks of this Court for his sermon on Wednes-
day last, and to desire him speedily to prepare
the same for the presse, adding thereto what he
had not time to deliver, the Court judging that the

---

[1] *New England Historical and Genealogical Register*, vol. VIII,
p. 20 ; Hutchinson's *History of Massachusetts*, vol. I, 1st and 2d ed.,
p. 141 ; 3d ed., p. 308.

[2] Lists of the preachers of the *Massachusetts Election Sermons*,
are printed in the appendix to the sermons of Revs. Samuel Deane,
1794, David Osgood, 1809, Andrew Bigelow, 1836, John Pierce,
1849, Alonzo H. Quint, 1866 and Charles E. Grinnell, 1871. The
list appended to Rev. Mr. Grinnell's sermon has been thoroughly
revised by Harry H. Edes of Charlestown, who has given in connection with it, much valuable information relative to the *Massachusetts Election Sermons*.

[3] Samuel Nowell.

printing of it will be for the publick benefitt."[1]
As the government was dissolved soon after, it is
possible that the sermon was never printed, though
in several lists of the election sermons that I have
seen, it is marked as having been printed.

Among his private memoranda, there are a
number of entries which show that he believed that,
at an early period in his ministry at Malden, there
was an unfriendly feeling towards him in the breasts
of many of the people there, especially among the
prominent citizens of the place. Perhaps ill health
may have made him more suspicious than the facts
would warrant; but I presume there was some
foundation for his belief. The position which he
occupied was a difficult one. A clergyman who is
called to fill the place of a brother who has been
forced to leave his pulpit against the wishes of a
large number of the congregation, is subjected to
many invidious comparisons. Mr. Matthews was
very popular in the town, and numbered among
his supporters most of the chief persons and a
majority of the voters there. It is probable that

---

[1] *Massachusetts Colony Records*, vol. v, pp. 514-15.

they sympathized with him in his religious views,
which are said to have been inclined to antinomian-
ism; and, as Mr. Wigglesworth's opinions seem
to have called forth no protest from the opponents
of his predecessor, we may infer that they were
satisfactory to them.   Under such circumstances,
it would not be surprising if the ardent friends of
Mr. Matthews should manifest a coolness towards
the person whom they were forced to hear.   The
ill health of Mr. Wigglesworth, which prevented
him from performing his duties as a minister to his
own satisfaction, was of a deceptive nature; and
this may have led some to think him negligent in
performing them.   But his absence, during his
brief residence in Bermuda, seems to have softened
the feeling towards him; and, on his return, he
met with a cordial reception from his parishioners.
This fact he gratefully records in his common-place
book.[1]

In one of the documents relating to Mr. Cheever's
case, there are intimations which lead me to think

---

[1] Ante, p. 75.

a disaffection towards him had again grown up, if it had ever been thoroughly eradicated. This belief is strengthened by the fact that for upwards of seven years after Mr. Cheever left, no salary was voted him by the town, though he was the only settled minister there. The disaffection may have grown out of his marriage, which according to Rev. Increase Mather, called forth censorious remarks.[1]

During the greater portion of his residence in Malden, that is while there was an associate minister settled there, there is reason to believe that Mr. Wigglesworth received no salary. In narrating his reception by his parishioners after his return from Bermuda, he says: " I have found more love from the people generally, both church and town, since my return then I did before; and they have done more for me of their own accord, when left to their liberty, then they had done for some years before I went away."[2] From this statement, I infer that he did not then consider that he had any claim upon the town for a salary. As the early

[1] Massachusetts Historical Collections, vol. XXXVIII, p. 94.
[2] Common-place Book.

town records are lost, there is no means of ascertaining what salary he received before his visit to
Bermuda; but it could not have been large or was
not promptly paid. The records commence December 30, 1678, and from that time till the dismission of Mr. Cheever, the only compensation for his
services which they record is a cartload of fire wood
voted him December 4, 1682,[1] while the salary of
Mr. Cheever was regularly voted and seems to have
been promptly paid during his continuance in
office.[2]

How Mr. Wigglesworth supported himself during
the early part of his sickness, after his return to
Malden, it is difficult to determine. It would seem
from his memorandum, made at a time when the
question was under consideration whether he should
be retained as the minister, about the year 1662,
that he then had little property.[3] It is not probable

---

[1] "4, 10, 82. Voted, that the Cutters and Carts in ye Towne cutt
& cart one load of fire wood for Mr Wigglesworth, on ye next
second day. Voted Corpl Jo. Green & Sergt Skinr overseers to
see ye wood cutt & carted."

[2] *Bi-Centennial Book of Malden*, p. 189.

[3] *Ante*, p. 61.

that he received much, after this, by inheritance.
Some income was probably obtained from the sale
of his books, and individual members of the parish
may have made him donations. Subsequently his
practise as a physician would be likely to procure
him a comfortable support, and he may also have
gained something, as ministers frequently did, by
teaching young men who were preparing for college
or the ministry. In 1677, we find Rev. Samuel
Hooker of Farmington, Ct., writing to Rev. Increase
Mather about the education of his son, who was
"indisposed" for the college, and using these words :
"I hear Mr. Wigglesworth, being at greater leisure
than som others (becaus of his rare preaching) is
thought a man very Idoneous for such instruction
as he needs."[1] From this it seems that his health
was supposed to be strong enough to enable him to
teach.

The result of the Council upon the state of the
Church of Malden, held in 1686, after advising, as
has been stated, that Mr. Cheever have a "Loving
Dismission," adds the following recommendation :

---

[1] *Massachusetts Historical Collections*, vol. xxxviii, p. 338.

" We advise the Church and Congregation of Malden duely to incourage and to hold in Reputation their Reverend and faithful Teacher Mr. Wigglesworth, according as God in his word does require them to do. 1 Thess. v, 12, 13. And that they conscientiously endeavour to live and Love as Brethren, forbearing one another, and forgiving one another, if any man have a quarrel against any, even as Christ forgave you, so also do yee." [1]

As Mr. Wigglesworth had never resigned his office of Teacher — a fact stated by himself in a letter to Samuel Sprague, dated July 22, 1687, which letter was extant in 1850,[2] — and as his health had been sufficiently restored to allow him to discharge the duties of his office, it would naturally be supposed that he would immediately resume the charge of the parish and that the town would settle a salary upon him, as it had done for Mr. Cheever while he officiated there. This was probably what the Council intended. But its advice does not

---

[1] Manuscript copy of *Result of Council* in the possession of D. P. Corey, Esq.

[2] *Bi-Centennial Book of Malden*, p. 156.

appear to have had the desired effect, for no provision was made by the town for his support. Cotton Mather gives the impression that he began to discharge the duties of his office as soon as his colleague left. " It pleased God " says he, " when the Distresses of the Church in Malden did extremely call for it, wondrously to Restore His Faithful Servant. He that had been for near Twenty years almost Buried Alive, comes abroad again ; and for as many years more, must in a Publick Usefulness receive the Answer and Harvest of the Thousands of Supplications with which the God of his Health had been addressed by him and for him." [1]

The following document shows, however, that the town had neglected its duties six months after the advice of the Council was given :

" NEW ENGLAND, ss.   By the President and Councell of his Majesties said territory and Dominion.

" Upon reading the petition of several inhabitants of Malden relateing to theyr ministry, &c.

---

[1] *Funeral Sermon,* p. 24.

" *Ordered.* That Mr. Deputy President, Capt. Winthrope and Mr. Wharton, members of his majesties Councell (with such other members of the Councell as can be present) with Mr. Increase Mather and Mr. Willard, be empowred a Comittee to repayr to Malden on tuesday next the 14th Instant, and to call before them the petitioners and other inhabitants of Malden, and to heare and finally determine and settle the maintenance of the ministry there, and that the Clerke of the Councell doe give forth a warrant to the Constables of Malden to warne a Generall Meeting att time and place accordingly.

" Given at the Councell house in Boston the 3d day of December, Anno R. R. Jacobi Anglie, &c., Secundo Annoq. Dom. 1686.

BEN. BULLIVANT, Clerke." [1]

What this committee did, I cannot learn. At the time the order was passed, Joseph Dudley, president of the Council, was the chief magistrate of

---

[1] Manuscript copy of the document in the hands of D. P. Corey, Esq

this jurisdiction. On the 20th of that month, Gov. Andros arrived, and a new order of affairs was inaugurated, which may have stayed the proceedings in this case.

The first mention of Mr. Wigglesworth on the town records after the departure of his colleague, is on the sixth of March, 1682–3, over six years after, as follows : " The 21 of this Instant, March, is apointed to cut and cart wood for Mr. Wigglesworth."[1] A similar vote was passed Jan. 24, 1693–4.

About seven weeks after the last vote, the proper provision for the support of the ministry was made. On the twelfth of March, 1693–4, it was " Voted. That the town will alow Mr. Wigglesworth fifty-five pounds a yeer yeerly In money, And the use of the passonage, and a suficant suply of fierwood, so Long as He carrieth one the work of the ministrey ; the yeere begineth the 12 of March, 1694."[2] It was also " voted that Mr. Wigglesworth shall haue Thirty cord of Cordwood Laid at his dore for this present yeer."[3]

---

[1] *Records of Malden.* These extracts have been furnished me by D. P. Corey, Esq., of Malden.   [2] *Ibid.*   [3] *Ibid.*

The delay of the town in recognizing him as their minister, by voting him a salary, may have been partly owing to an apprehension that by so doing they would render themselves liable to him for past services. A whimsical document on the town books, signed by Mr. Wigglesworth about two years after a salary had been voted him, gives plausibility to this conjecture. It reads as follows:

" These lines are to let all men understand That I, Michael Wigglesworth of Malden, doe Herby discharg And Acquit the Town of Malden from all claimes that may be made heerafter by my self my haires executors Administrators or a signes upon the acount of aney Salary debt or dues to me for the work of the ministery from the beginning of The world until the 12 of March 1694–5. In witness of the primeses, I have hereunto set my hand and seall this 28 of March 1695–6.

MICHAEL WIGGLESWORTH " [SEAL.].[1]

The body of this document, with its uncouth spelling, is in the handwriting of the town clerk.

_____

[1] _Bi-Centennial Book of Malden_, p. 190.

It will be noticed that no consideration is mentioned in it.

In 1696, Mr. Wigglesworth's compensation was fixed at Fifty pounds and the stranger's money ; and he received some years thirty-five instead of thirty cords of wood.[1]   On the 31st of March, 1698, it was voted, "That the town will aford Mr. Wigglesworth sum help 4 or 5 sabath days in the work of the minestry." [2]

After his death, March 8, 1705–6, the following vote was passed : " Voted that Mrs. Wigglesworth haue alowed her 4 shillings per week for her entertaining the ministers sinc Mr. Wigglesworth decesed, which is 30 weeks." It was also voted " that Mrs. Wigglesworth shall haue £12.10.0, money paid her for Mr. Wigglesworth's Labour in the ministrey the last quarter of a yeer he lived." [3]   On the third of October, 1707, the town finds itself still indebted to Mrs. Wigglesworth £12. 1s. 7d., on arrears of her husband's salary.[4]

Previous to his voyage to Bermuda in 1663, Mr. Wigglesworth resided, I presume, in the parsonage,

[1] *Records of Malden, in loco.*   [2] *Ibid.*   [3] *Ibid.*
[4] *Bi-Centennial Book of Malden,* p. 190.

or, as it is sometimes called, the "ministry house."
The land on which this house stood was purchased
by the town under a vote December 22, 1651, and
the house was erected previous to June, 1655. In
this house, it is likely, the *Day of Doom* was written.
On the last day of December, 1657, Mr. Wigglesworth bought an estate of his own to the eastward
of the parsonage land and adjoining it. It consisted
of six and a half acres of land and remained in his
possession at the time of his death. Here he probably resided after his return from Bermuda till
the town voted him the use of the parsonage in the
spring of 1694; and here, without much doubt,
Meat out of the Eater was composed. Both of the
houses were destroyed by fire early in the last century, the parsonage having been burnt on the 31st
of July, 1724, and the mansion house that had been
owned by Mr. Wigglesworth on the 9th of August,
1730.[1] The remains of two cellars which Mr.
Corey thinks are those of the two houses in which
the author of the *Day of Doom* resided, were visible
within the memory of persons now living.

---

[1] *Bi-Centennial Book of Malden*, pp. 191 and 128.

Less than two years after the death of his wife Martha, Mr. Wigglesworth was again married. His new wife was Mrs. Sybil Avery, widow of Dr. Jonathan Avery, a physician of Dedham, Massachusetts. The precise time of this marriage is unknown, but it was subsequent to March 23, 1691. Two letters written to Mrs. Avery during their courtship are preserved, the latest of which bears this date. The letters are both printed in the *New England Historical and Genealogical Register.*[1] Mrs. Avery was a daughter of Nathaniel Sparhawk of Cambridge. She was born about the year 1655, and consequently was about seven years older than his previous wife, though more than twenty years younger than he. She belonged to a family of some distinction in the colony, and was beloved for her kind and charitable disposition. Her character and standing in society may have aided her husband in allaying the troubles in his parish.

A silver locket in the form of a heart, which once belonged to her, and a silver box made for keeping it in, having passed in separate lines to her

---

[1] Vol. XVII, pp. 139 to 142.

descendants, were brought together in a singular
manner, after being separated for three generations.
A description of these relics and the circumstances
attending their reunion written by Rev. Andrew P.
Peabody, D.D., of Harvard University, was printed
in the *Christian Register*, June 1st, 1850.[1]

On the 13th of October, 1690, a meeting of the
ministers of Boston and vicinity was held at Charlestown at which an association was formed. The
idea was taken from the United Brethren, a recent
London organization. Rev. Charles Morton the first
signer had come from England a few years previous, and was probably in correspondence with the
London Independent and Presbyterian ministers
who formed the English association; and Rev. Increase Mather, the father of another signer, was then
in England and active in promoting that union.[2] Rev.
Mr. Wigglesworth was the third signer of the articles of association.[3] The meetings of the United
Ministers, as they were styled, were held monthly,

---

[1] See *New England Historical and Genealogical Register*, IV, 186
[2] Cotton Mather's *Magnalia*, bk. v. pp. 58–9.
[3] The articles are printed in *New England Historical and Genealogical Register*, and Mather's *Magnalia*, ubi supra.

except in winter, in the library of Harvard College.
This was the first attempt in New England by the
clergy to hold stated meetings for consultation though
they had been in the habit of discussing religious
questions when they met at the weekly lectures.[1]

In the terrible Witchcraft delusion of 1692, I
have found no evidence that he took an active part
on either side. Mr. Upham after mentioning that
his church was invited to the *ex parte* council called
by Rev. Mr. Parris, remarks: "From the tone of
his writings, it is quite probable that he favored the
witchcraft proceedings at the beginning; but the
change of mind, afterwards strongly expressed, had,
perhaps, then begun to be experienced, for he did
not respond to the call, as his name does not appear
in the record of the Council." [2] After the delusion
had passed away he united with other clergymen
in allaying the troubles which it had occasioned.[3]
The summer previous to his death, while the colony
was sorely afflicted, he wrote a letter to his friend,

---

[1] Cotton Mather's *Thirty Important Cases*, (1699) preface.

[2] *Salem Witchcraft and Cotton Mather*, p. 65.

[3] *New England Historical and Genealogical Register*, vol. XI, pp. 319–20.

Rev. Increase Mather, in which he attributes the sufferings of the people from the drought and from the long continued war they were then engaged in, to a judgment of God for the innocent blood shed in those melancholly times; and urges a public and solemn humiliation of the people — particularly of those who were active in the matter — for the wrong; and that amends and reparation should be made by the government to the families of the sufferers.[1] This was seven years after Judge Sewall had made his famous public confession, January 14, 1696-7.[2]

In 1696, he preached the sermon before the Artillery Company at its annual election. At the time he was invited to preach this sermon, an attendant on his ministry, Col. Nicholas Paige, a wealthy Boston merchant, was the captain of the company, having been chosen at the election the previous year. The favorite residence of Col. Paige was at Rumney Marsh, since Chelsea, where he owned a farm. " While residing there, he attended

---

[1] See *Massachusetts Historical Collections*, vol. XXXVIII, pp. 645-7.

[2] *New England Historical and Genealogical Register*, vol. XXIV, pp. 412-13, *note*.

worship in Malden, which was more easy of access than Boston."[1] It was no doubt at the instance of Col. Paige that his pastor was invited to preach the annual sermon before the Artillery Company. The sermon was not printed.

He was visited with a severe fit of sickness about seven years before his death. His people who had now learned his worth were alarmed by his illness. They came together, according to Mather, with agony. They prayed and fasted, and wept before the Lord, with public supplications for his life. Their prayer was granted; and he was spared to minister for a few years longer, to their spiritual and bodily wants.[2] About the time of this sickness, March 31, 1698, the town voted him a short respite from his labors.[3] I presume this was after his

---

[1] *Bi-Centennial Book of Malden*, p. 127. The town, March 14th, 1692, passed a vote that "Corronal page hath liberty to build a pew." In 1701, he presented to the church an elegant pair of silver chalices which have been preserved to our own times.

[2] Mather's *Funeral Sermon*, p. 25.

[3] "Voted y^t ye town will aford Mr. Wigglesworth sum help 4 or 5 sabath days in ye work of ye ministry." *Malden Records*, March 31, 1698.

recovery, but while he was still feeble from the effects of his illness.

At length his last sickness came. He was attacked with a fever which in ten days terminated fatally. He died at nine o'clock in the morning on Sunday the tenth of June, 1705.[1] His youngest son, Edward, who was a youth, twelve or thirteen years of age, when he died, recorded, six years after, this account of his death : " It pleased the Almighty disposer of all things, in his wise Providence, to take from my head him who should have been the guide of my youth, causing my father to rest from his labors on the Lord's-day, June the 10th, 1705. Before he died, he gave me his blessing, and then left this solemn charge with me. ' Thou, my son, know thou the God of thy fathers and serve him with a perfect heart and with a willing mind. If thou

[1] Chief Justice Sewall in his *Common-place Book* thus records his death : " Lord's Day, June 10, 1705. The Learned and pious Mr. Michael Wigglesworth dies at Malden ab¹ 9 m. Had been sick ab¹ 10 days of a Fever ; 73 years and 8 moneths old. He was the Author of the Poem entituled, *The Day of Doom*, which has been so often printed ; and was very usefull as a Physician." *American Quarterly Register*, vol. xi, p. 193.

seek him, he will be found of thee, but if thou
forsake him, he will cast thee off forever.'   A charge
which I have reason, at this time, to reflect upon
with fear and trembling."[1]

Though, for a great portion of his life, he had
suffered from ill health, yet he lived to a ripe old
age.   At his death, he wanted but a few months of
completing his seventy-fourth year.   He survived
all his classmates, at Harvard College, except one,
living more than half a century after his graduation,
and seeing the infant institution at which he was
educated honored and loved by a land which it had
rescued from ignorance if not barbarism.   Of the
forty-three graduates in the classes which preceded
his own, few were living when he died.

Rev. Cotton Mather preached a sermon at Malden
on his life and character the second Sunday after
his death.   The sermon was printed, at Boston,
the same year, with a dedication by the Rev. Increase Mather, the preacher's father, to the church
and congregation at Malden, and an appendix con-

---

[1] Statement of Edward Wigglesworth, written in one of his
father's common-place books, in the year 1711.

taining a selection from the manuscripts left by Mr. Wigglesworth, concluding with a punning epitaph by "one who had been gratified by his *Meat out of the Eater* and *Day of Doom.*" This epitaph is generally ascribed to Cotton Mather himself and probably correctly.[1]

In the autumn of 1849, nearly a century and a half after the first issue, the sermon was reprinted at Boston under the editorship of the late Rev. Alexander W. McClure, D.D., at the instance and chiefly at the expense of Mrs. Dolly (Blanchard) Upham, an aged matron of Malden, who died several years ago. In the title pages of this edition

---

[1] " A Faithful Man Described and Rewarded. Some Observable and Serviceable Passages in the Life and Death of Mr. Michael Wigglesworth, Late Pastor of Malden ; Who Rested from his Labours on the Lord's-Day, June 10th, 1705, In the Seventy Fourth year of his Age. And Memorials of Piety, Left behind him among his Written Experiences.— With a Funeral Sermon, Preached (for him) at Malden, June 24, 1705. By Cotton Mather.

> Factitium Vobis Sermonem in Omni forma
> Sanctitatis Dei Servus Exhibuit.
> Ber. in obit. Humb.

Boston : Printed by B. Green for Benj. Eliot at his Shop under the West End of the Town-House, 1705." Post 8vo., pp. 6 and 48.

the sermon is erroneously attributed to Rev. Increase
Mather.[1]

Mr. Wigglesworth determined early in life to
discharge with faithfulness the duties belonging to
his position, and strength was given him to accom-
plish much for the good of his fellow men. He
died respected for his talents, and honored for his
virtues. "As he was Faithful to the Death," to

---

[1] *A Faithful Man Described and Rewarded.* A Sermon Preached
at Malden, June 24, 1705, occasioned by the Death of that Faithful
and Aged Servant of God, Mr. Michael Wigglesworth. By Increase
Mather, D.D., Pastor of the North Church in Boston. Boston ;
Republished by John Putnam, 81 Cornhill, 1849." 12mo, pp. 52.

I presume that this edition was reprinted from a copy with the
title-page missing. As the dedication is signed by Increase Mather
and the name of Cotton Mather is not found in the book except on
the title-page, it would be natural for a person who had a copy
with the title-page wanting to suppose the sermon to have been
preached by Increase Mather.

The title-page of the reprint seems to have been made up by
Rev. Dr. McClure by copying the half-title at the beginning of the
sermon in the first edition and adding the name and office of the
supposed author. It is a literal reprint of the half-title, except
that " Malden " in the reprint is " Maldon " in the original ; " on "
is omitted in the reprint before "June ;" and " Departure " is changed
to " Death." McClure probably wrote from memory (*Book of
Malden*, p. 154), in regard to an anonymous edition in 1705.

quote the words of Mather, "so he was Lively to the Death. He earnestly desired, That he might hold out, Useful unto the Last. God granted him his Desire; A Desire seldom denied unto them that are so Importunate in it. It was a surprize unto us, to see a Little Feeble Shadow of a Man beyond Seventy, Preaching usually Twice or Thrice in a Week: Visiting and Comforting the Afflicted; Encouraging the Private Meetings; Catechising the Children of the Flock; and managing the Government of the Church; and attending the Sick, not only in his own Town, but also in all those of the Vicinity. Thus he did, unto the Last; and he was but one Lords-Day taken off before his Last. But in the Last Week of his Life, how full of Resignation; how full of Satisfaction!"[1]

Peirce, in his *History of Harvard University*, states that at the Commencement succeeding his death, which this year fell on the fourth of July, " young Holyoke who was afterwards President,[2] pronounced

---

[1] Mather's *Funeral Sermon*, pp. 25-6.

[2] Rev. Edward Holyoke, H. C., 1705, was president from 1737 to 1769.

the Bachelor's oration, and made respectful mention of this deceased minister, styling him ' MALDO-NATUS ORTHODOXUS.' " [1]

A moss-covered gravestone, in the old burial ground at Malden, indicates the place where, more than a century and a half ago, his weeping parishioners laid the remains of their venerated pastor and friend. On it the following inscription [2] is still legible :

```
        MEMENTO           FUGIT
        MORI.             HORA.
    HERE   LYES   BURIED   Yᴱ   BODY   OF
    THAT   FAITHFULL   SERUANT   OF
    JESUS   CHRIST   Yᴱ   REUEREND
    Mᴿ   MICHAEL   WIGGLESWORTH
    PASTOUR OF  Yᴱ   CHURCH OF CHRIST
    AT   MAULDEN         YEARS   WHO
    FINNISHED  HIS  WORK  AND  ENTRᴱᴰ
    APON  AN  ETERNAL  SABBATH
    OF  REST  ON  Yᴱ   LORDS  DAY  IUNE
    Yᴱ  10  1705  IN  Yᴱ  74 YEAR OF HIS AGE.

    HERE  LIES  INTERD  IN  SILENT  GRAUᴱ
    BELOW           MAULDENS   PHYSICIAN
       FOR   SOUL   AND   BODY   TWO.
```

[1] Peirce's *History of Harvard University*, p. 251. The term " *Maldonatus* " is evidently applied to Wigglesworth in allusion not only to his residence, but also, as Rev. Dr. McClure suggests (*Bi-Centennial Book of Malden*, p. 155), to the Spanish jesuit, Johannes Maldonatus, who was celebrated for his learning and piety.

[2] The inscription in the text is printed from the *Historical and Genealogical Register*, vol. XIX, p. 36. Mr. Corey, who copied it

"The late Deacon Ramsdell," says Mr. McClure,
" out of pious reverence for his memory, was
accustomed once a year, like ' Old Mortality ' in the
Tales of My Landlord, to refresh this time-worn
inscription. It seems to be time," he continues,
" that some monument more fitting than that crum-
bling and almost illegible and invisible stone should
mark the spot where his ashes rest." [1]

He had eight children by his three wives, namely,
two sons and six daughters, all of whom survived
him and through whom he has a numerous posterity.
The births of all of his children except the youngest
are on record at Malden. His first wife, Mary,
left but one child, Mercy, born in February, 1655–6.
His wife Martha had five daughters and one son,
Abigail, born March 20, 1680–1 ; Mary, September
21, 1682 ; Martha, December, 1683 ; Esther, April
16, 1685 ; Dorothy, February 22, 1686–7 ; and

---

for the *Register*, states that there are some mistakes in the copy in
the *Bi-Centennial Book of Malden*, p. 154, which have been corrected in his. The space in the 8th line, between " Maulden " and
" Years," was left blank when the stone was lettered.

[1] *Bi-Centennial Book of Malden*, p. 154.

Samuel, February 4,, 1688–9. His last wife, Sybil, had one son, Edward, born about the year 1692.

The eldest daughter, Mercy, married Samuel Brackenbury, who graduated at Harvard College in 1664, preached two years at Rowley, but was not ordained, afterwards removed to Boston, where he practiced as a physician and died in January, 1678. She afterwards married Rev. Samuel Belcher, a graduate of Harvard in the class of 1659, who preached for a time at the Isles of Shoals and was ordained, at Newbury, Nov. 10, 1698. He died at Ipswich, his native town, March 10, 1714–15, aged 74. She survived him and died Nov. 14, 1723.

His second daughter, Abigail,[1] married Samuel Tappan of Newbury. They had eight children, the youngest of whom was Rev. Benjamin Tappan of Manchester, Mass., who died May 6, 1794, at the age of 74, and after a ministry of about forty-five years.[2] Among their descendants may be named,

---

[1] A letter from her to her son Benjamin, written in 1740, while he was at College is printed in the *Memoir of Mrs. Sarah Tappan* (1834), pp. 133–5.

[2] A list of the children and grandchildren of his son Benjamin (who married Sarah Homes, whose memoir is referred to in the preceding note), is printed in that memoir, pp. 129–132.

Rev. David Tappan, professor of Divinity at Harvard College from 1792 to 1803; Rev. Amos Tappan of Kingston, N. H.; Hon. Benjamin Tappan, United States Senator from Ohio from 1839 to 1845; Arthur and Lewis Tappan of New York; John and Charles Tappan of Boston; Henry Edwards of Boston; Hon. Ebenezer Bradbury of Newburyport; John M. Bradbury of Boston; Rev. Benjamin Tappan, D.D., of Augusta, Me.,[1] and the wives of Rev. John Pierce, D.D., Rev. Calvin Durfee, D.D., Rev. Frederic H. Hedge, D.D., Rev. Thomas B. Fox, and Rev. Edwin B. Webb, D.D.

His third daughter, Mary, was living March 31, 1708, and bore at that time the name of Wigglesworth.

His fourth daughter, Martha, married a Mr. Wheeler, after whose death she married Samuel Law, a physician, and died at Stonington, Ct., Dec. 4, 1719. Her last husband died at Groton, Ct., April 30, 1727, in his 47th year. She had a son, by Mr. Wheeler or a previous husband, living

---

[1] The descendants of Rev. Benjamin Tappan, D.D., are given in North's *History of Augusta, Maine*, pp. 943-4.

March 31, 1708, and had two children by Dr. Law, namely: Wigglesworth, born February 1, 1716–7, and Martha, born Nov. 27, 1719, who died March 12, 1719–20, a few months after her own death.[1]

His fifth daughter, Esther, married June 8, 1708, John Sewall of Newbury, who died in 1711. She married secondly, Abraham Tappan of the same town October 21, 1713. More than five hundred of her descendants, through her son Edward Tappan of Newbury, are given in the *Toppans of Toppans Lane*, by Joshua Coffin (Newburyport, 1862), pp. 13 to 28. The list includes Joshua Coffin, the historian of Newbury, and author of the *Toppans of Toppans Lane;* and Edward Little, a graduate of Dartmouth College in 1797, who published the 1811 edition of the *Day of Doom.* Among her other descendants are Hon. Thomas Rice, member of Congress from 1815 to 1819, the writer of this memoir, and the wife of Rev. John Wheelock Allen.

His youngest daughter, Dorothy, married June 2, 1709, James Upham of Malden. Among their

---

[1] *New England Historical and Genealogical Register*, vol. xxiii, p. 212

descendants are Rev. Edward Upham, Hon. Benjamin F. Wade, United States Senator from Ohio,
from 1851 to 1869, his brother, Edward, a member
of the House from the same state, and his niece
Nellie, wife of Hon. Schuyler Colfax, vice president
of the United States.[1]

His two youngest children were sons. The elder
of these, Rev. Samuel Wigglesworth, was graduated
at Harvard College in 1707. After practising
medicine, teaching school and preaching several
years, he was ordained over the church at Ipswich
Hamlet, now Hamilton, October 27, 1714, where he
continued the pastor till his death, September 3,
1768, at the age of 79. He married first, Mary
Brintnal of Winnesimmet, now Chelsea, June 30,
1715. She died June 6, 1723, and he married March
12, 1730, Martha Brown of Reading, who survived
him and died in November, 1784, at Newburyport.[2]

---

[1] The descendants of James Wade, who married Mary, daughter
of Rev. Edward Upham, are given in Brooks's *History of Medford*,
pp. 557-60. See also *New England Historical and Genealogical
Register*, vol. XXIII, pp. 35 and 38.

[2] A sketch of his life with a list of his publications, will be found
in Felt's *History of Ipswich*, pp. 279-83.

He had thirteen children. His third son, Edward, graduated at Harvard College in 1761, was a colonel in the Revolutionary army and United States collector at Newburyport.[1]

The youngest child of Michael Wigglesworth was, Prof. Edward Wigglesworth, D.D., who graduated at Harvard in 1710. For a time he was usher of a grammar school in Boston, but left the employment with the design of settling in the ministry. He took chambers at the college, lived there and preached occasionally till June 28, 1721, when he was unanimously elected at the age of thirty, the first Hollis professor of Divinity. He was inaugurated as such October 24, 1722, and held the office, with high respect for his learning and piety, upwards of forty years. He was a fellow of the corporation. The degree of D.D., was given to him by Edinburgh University. He died at Cambridge, January 16, 1765, in the 73d year of his age,[2] and was succeeded as Hollis Professor by his son, Prof. Edward

[1] A sketch of his life is given in Mrs. Smith's *History of Newburyport*, pp. 356–62.

[2] A list of his publications is given in the notice of him in Allen's *American Biographical Dictionary*.

Wigglesworth, D.D., who held the office from 1765 till 1791, when his health failing he was succeeded by his relative Rev. David Tappan, also a descendant of the author of the *Day of Doom*. "It is a very remarkable circumstance," says Rev. Dr. McClure, writing in 1850, "that of the four Hollis Professors, 'the three first, who held the chair for eighty successive years, with high reputation, should have been respectively the son, grandson and great-grandson of that good man." The eldest daughter of the second Hollis Professor, was Margaret, wife of Rev. John Andrews of Newburyport.[1] Thomas Wigglesworth, her youngest brother, graduated at Harvard College in 1793, and was the father of Edward Wigglesworth, an assistant editor of the *Encyclopædia Americana*.[2]

Mrs. Sybil Wigglesworth survived her husband a little over three years, having died August 6, 1708, in the 54th year of her age. She was buried at

---

[1] See preface to Autobiography, APPENDIX I.

[2] See Bond's *Genealogies and History of Watertown*, pp. 171 and 176, for a genealogical account of the descendants of the first Prof. Edward Wigglesworth.

Cambridge, where her gravestone is still standing.[1] After the death of her husband, she resided at the parsonage in Malden till the following spring, as is shown by votes of the town. She soon after removed to Cambridge, her native place, and the town voted July 29, 1706, to pay her for the improvements at the parsonage made by her husband.

Her son, writing a few years after her death, describes her as "an affectionate, charitable, praying saint, one who desired the good of everybody, and likewise to be herself ever doing in good." He adds that she "endured many sorrows and underwent great afflictions, in all which she was a mirrour of patience and constancy, bearing all with true Christian fortitude, till at length God took her from a sinful and weary world to joy unspeakable and full of glory."[2]

The character of Rev. Michael Wigglesworth himself is thus given by his son in the writing just quoted: "My Father was eminent for Learning

---

[1] The inscription on it is printed in Harris's *Cambridge Epitaphs,* p. 40.

[2] Manuscript statement of Edward Wigglesworth, 1711, before quoted.

and holiness, for fidelity and constancy in his en-
deavours to serve God and benefit his people to the
utmost of his Ability in some capacity or other
amidst those manifold afflictions, difficulties and
inconveniences which he laboured under for the
greatest part of his Life, and amidst which had not
his confidence been in the Lord and his relyance
upon the power of his might for rightcousness and
for strength, his hands could never have been strong,
nor his heart been able to endure; but his hope
was in the Almighty arm of the merciful Jehovah,
and it made him not ashamed : for the Lord was
with him in six troubles, yea, and in seven he sus-
tained him, and brought him to see peace in his
Latter End." [1]

Rev. Andrew P. Peabody, D.D., University
preacher at Harvard College, a decided opponent
of his theological views, in writing of him, says :
" He was, it is believed, notwithstanding his repul-
sive creed, ' a man of the beatitudes,' a physician
to the bodies no less than to the souls of his parishioners, genial and devotedly kind in the relations

---

[1] Statement of Edward Wigglesworth, 11.

and duties of his social and professional life, and distinguished, even in those days of abounding sanctity, for the singleness and purity of heart that characterized his whole walk and conversation." [1]

Frederic S. Hill states that he was " respected in the pulpit for his modest, though lucid exposition of the scriptures; esteemed in the social circle for the suavity of his manners; and beloved by many to whom, in their youth, he had been the faithful friend and counsellor." [2]

Benjamin Peirce, librarian of Harvard College, asserts in the book before quoted, that he was " greatly esteemed as an able, a sound and a pious divine, and as a skillful physician for the body as well as the soul ; " and that " he possessed moreover the talent of interesting his devout contemporaries by his poetical effusions." [3]

The poet at the bi-centennial celebration at Malden, May 23, 1849, thus introduces him to his hearers, and touches upon some points of his character :

---

[1] *Christian Register*, June 1, 1850.

[2] Kettell's *Specimens of American Poetry*, vol. I, p. 35.

[3] *History of Harvard University*, p. 251.

"Soon there appeared a poet. whose great shade
Perhaps inspires the verses we have made,
Who wove. in sickness, on dark Fancy's loom.
The varied aspects of the ' Day of Doom ; '
Which wandering down the ages. yet remains
Fair sample of our Fathers' kind of brains,
This famous poet could, with equal skill,
Wield harp or scalpel.—form a rhyme or pill ;
And not alone could bend each stubborn word
By rhythmic music into sweet accord.
Not only oft their slight diseases healed
By balms which harmless herbs and roots may yield —
The Sabbath was to him no day of rest :
From sacred pulpits he. to souls distrest.
Prescribed prescriptions. very long but good,
Which would restore the dying multitude.
In yonder spot his grave you yet may view,
And read his epitaph so quaint and true.
Maulden's physician for soul and body too.' " [1]

Of those writers whose character of Mr. Wigglesworth have been quoted in this memoir. three only,
namely: his son Edward and Rev. Increase and

---

[1] Poem delivered at Malden. May 23, 1849. by Gilbert Haven, Jr.,
printed in Bi-Centennial Book of Malden. p. 75. Whittier introduces Wigglesworth into *Margaret Smith's Diary*, pp. 208–11 :
but he does not attempt to describe his person or character. as they
were pictured in his fancy

Cotton Mather. speak of him from a personal knowledge. More or less imagination must, of course, be mixed up with the descriptions of later writers. The following extracts from Sabbath memoranda made by him during the early part of his ministry, which Rev. Dr. McClure prints in his biographical sketch, have a higher value than even the testimony of contemporaries. They show, to use the words of Dr. McClure, " his eminent spirituality of mind and his heavenly zeal." [1]

"1658, March 21. Oh how vehemently do I desire to serve God, and not myself, in the conversion of souls this day. My soul longs after thy hous and work, O God!"

"Jan. 9, '58 [1658–9]. My soul panteth after thee O God! After more of thy favor, more of thyne image. O satisfy me with the fatnes of thy hous make me to drink of the rivers of thy joys, that for outward presures, I may have inward supportings and consolations. *Tibi Christe servire cupio ; opitularem.*"

---

[1] *Bi-Centennial Book of Malden*, p. 147.

" Feb. 6.   My soul be cheerful in thy work; thou servest a good Master."

" June 5.   Now in the strength of Christ, I desire to seek him, and the advancement of his glory in the salvation of souls this day. * * * Oh my soul, perform this labor as thy last."

" Sept. 25.

> " My sins and wants stil sorely pain my heart;
> My hope in Christ relieves my smart,
> And in his day and work, I do delight." [1]

Of his skill as a physician we have no record; but one of the favorite medicines of the famous Dr. Holyoke of Salem, that known as the " Balsam of Fennel," is said to have been previously used by Mr. Wigglesworth. I presume that Dr. Holyoke obtained the recipe from Rev. Samuel Wigglesworth, probably while he was studying medicine with Dr. Berry of the neighboring parish of Ipswich.[2]

---

[1] Mr Wigglesworth's common-place book.

[2] See Memoir of Edward A. Holyoke, M.D., LL.D. (Boston 1826) pp. 20-1. The recipe for this medicine is given in full in the Appendix, pp. 68-9.

A catalogue of his library will be printed in this volume.[1] By his will he left all his books to his two sons, to be divided between them after his wife had chosen half a dozen English books. The catalogue will, I feel assured, be appreciated by all who take an interest in the man or his writings. Next to the books which an author composes may be placed those which he reads as an index to his mind; and, as a general rule, we may infer that the books he possesses are those which he reads. True, it is not always safe to judge of a man's mental tastes by the contents of his library; for one sometimes comes into the possession, by gift or otherwise, of works in which he has little, if any, interest; but such books are not often sufficiently numerous to affect the character of a library of even moderate dimensions.

Though we may not be able to select from Mr. Wigglesworth's books those which he chose as the special companions of his solitude and

---

[1] It is printed in APPENDIX III, from his inventory among the Middlesex Probate files at EastCambridge, Mass.

study, yet we can form some conjecture upon the subject from the character of the collection, which is obvious to all. This, with the tone of his writings, will enable us to form a tolerably accurate judgment as to his predilections. The list will also be of service by showing us the books read by the clergy of New England in the latter half of the seventeenth century, and by indicating some of the subjects which engrossed their thoughts.

The library is eminently a practical one, consisting largely of books useful for reference ; and seems to have been chosen to fit its owner for his duties as a preacher and a physician. It is rich in works upon theology and history; and there is also a good collection of medical books. Of classical literature there is little, and of English *belles-lettres* nothing. But what will excite most surprise is the dearth of poetry. Not even the poems of Mrs. Bradstreet, the pride of New England ; nor of " Silver-tongued Sylvester," so much in repute with the Puritans of the preceding age; nor of zealous John Bunyan, a truly fraternal spirit ; nor the grand epic of Milton,

on a subject kindred to his own, are there.[1] A
solitary volume — and that by an author whose
polished verses and sportive wit bear little resem-
blance to his own rugged rhymes and sombre fancy —
comprises his whole poetical library. But even
this absence of his brethren of the lyre is signifi-
cant. From them Wigglesworth borrowed little.
In truth, he seems to have been more familiar with
the commentaries and theological treatises with
which his library abounded, than with the poets of
his own or other nations. Not that his style is
wholly prosaic, for there are passages in his writings which are truly poetical, both in thought and
expression, and which show that he was capable of
attaining a higher position as a poet than can now
be claimed for him. The roughness of his verses
was surely not owing to carelessness nor to indolence,
for neither of them were characteristic of the man.
The true explanation may be that he sacrificed his

---

[1] Neither the *Day of Doom* nor *Meat out of the Eater* is found in
the inventory. It may be worth noting that the catalogue of
Harvard College library, printed in 1723, does not contain either
of them.

poetic taste to his theology, and that for the sake
of inculcating sound doctrine he was willing to
write in halting numbers.

The author of the *Day of Doom*, though belonging to the straitest sect of Puritans, was, as has before
been said, a man of generous feelings towards his
fellows. Obedience to the supreme law gave a
heavenly lustre to his example and a sweet fragrance
to his memory. Such characters were not uncom-
mon among his contemporaries. The clergy of that
day possessed a deep religious earnestness and a
fervent piety. They were bible students and men
of prayer. Even many who consider them errone-
ous in doctrine are willing to allow that they were
strict in morals; that if wrong in faith, they were
right in life ; that, if their creed was opaque, their
hearts were luminous; and that, if their vision
did not discern the additional light which the saintly
Robinson had prophesied was yet to break forth
from God's word, they sincerely accepted what
light they saw. They were patient, hopeful, humble,
believing, faithful. They stood on a higher plane
than their successors, and exercised a proportionably

higher power over their hearers. Their people revered them, were constant in attendance on their services, and submitted gladly to their sway.

APPENDIX.

I.

AUTOBIOGRAPHY.

The following autobiographic sketch of the early life of Rev. Michael Wigglesworth is printed from a copy made in the winter of 1863, from the original then in the possession of a daughter of Rev. John Andrews, D.D., of Newburyport, Mass. It was borrowed for me by my friend William Reed Deane, Esq. Miss Andrews, who has since died, resided at Newburyport. She was descended from the author of the *Day of Doom*, through her mother, a daughter of Rev. Edward Wigglesworth, Jr., D.D., the second Hollis Professor of Divinity in Harvard College. She had other interesting relics of her ancestor.

Rev. Dr. McClure suggests that the autobiography was probably prepared "to be presented at his examination as a candidate for ordination;"[1] and as the narrative closes a about that period, I am inclined to adopt this opinion. The document was first printed in the *Christian Register*, an Unitarian newspaper, printed at Boston, June 29, 1850, from a copy made by Rev. Andrew P. Peabody, D.D., LL.D.

---

[1] *Bi-Centennial Book of Malden*, p. 144.

It was next printed by me in the *New England Historical and Genealogical Register*, vol. XVII, pp. 137–9.

I was born of Godly Parents, that feared ye Lord greatly, even from their youth, but in an ungodly Place, where ye generality of ye people rather derided then imitated their piety, in a place where, to my knowledge, their children had Learnt wickedness betimes; In a place that was consumed wth fire in a great part of it, after God had brought them out of it. These Godly parents of mine meeting with opposition & persecution for Religion, because they went from their own Parish Church to hear ye word & Receiv ye L^s supper, &c., took up resolutions to pluck vp their stakes & remove themselves to New England, and accordingly they did so, Leaving dear Relations friends & acquaintāce, their native Land, a new built house, a flourishing Trade, to expose themselves to ye hazzard of ye seas, and to ye Distressing difficulties of a howling wilderness, that they might enjoy Liberty of Conscience & Christ in his ordinances. And the Lord brought them hither & Landed them at Charlstown, after many difficulties and hazzards, and me along with them being then a child not full seven years old. After about 7 weeks stay at Charls Town, my parents removed again by sea to New-Haven in ye month of October. In o^r passage thither we were in great Danger by a storm which drove us upon a Beach of sand where we lay beating til another Tide fetcht us off; but God carried us to o^r port in safety. Winter approaching we dwelt in a Cellar partly under ground covered

with earth the first winter. But I remember that one great
rain brake in upon us & drencht me so in my bed being
asleep that I fell sick upon it; but ye Lord in mercy spar'd
my life & restored my health. When ye next summer was
come I was sent to school to Mr. Ezekiel Cheever who at
that time taught school in his own house, and under him in
a year or two I profited so much through ye blessing of God,
that I began to make Latin & to get forward apace. But
God who is infinitely wise and absolutely soverain, and gives
no account concerning any of his proceedings, was pleased
about this time to visit my Father with Lameness which
grew upon him more & more to his dying Day, though he
Liv'd under it 13 yeers. He wanting help was fain to take
me off from school to follow other employments for ye space
of 3 or 4 yeers until I had lost all that I had gained in the
Latine Tongue. But when I was now in my fourteenth
yeer, my Father, who I suppose was not wel satisfied in
keeping me from Learning whereto I had been designed
from my infancy, & not judging me fit for husbandry, sent
me to school again, though at that time I had little or no
disposition to it, but I was willing to submit to his authority
therein and accordingly I went to school under no small
disadvantage & discouragement seing those that were far
inferior to me, by my discontinuance now gotten far before
me. But in a little time it appeared to be of God, who was
pleased to facilitate my work & bless my studies that I soon
recovered what I had lost & gained a great deal more, so
that in 2 yeers & 3 quarters I was judged fit for ye Colledge

18

and thither I was sent, far from my parents & acquaintāce among strangers. But when father & mother both forsook me then the Lord took care of me. It was an act of great self Denial in my father that notwithstanding his own Lameness & great weakness of Body wch required the service & helpfulness of a son, and having but one son to be ye staff of his age & supporter of his weakness he would yet for my good be content to deny himself of that comfort & Assistf ance I might have Lent him. It was also an evident proof of a strong Faith in him, in that he durst adventure to send me to ye Colledge, though his Estate was but small & little enough to maintain himself & small family left at home. And God Let him Live to see how acceptable to himselthis service was in giving up his only son to ye Lord and bringing him up to Learning, especially ye Lively actings of his faith & self denial herein. For first notwithstanding his great weakness of body, yet he Lived til I was so far brought up as that I was called to be a fellow of y^c Colledge and improved in Publick service there, and until I had preached several Times ; yea and more then so, he Lived to see & hear what God had done for my soul in turning me from Darkness to light & frō the power of Sathan unto God, wch filled his heart ful of joy and thankfulness beyond what can be expressed. And for his outward estate, that was so far from being sunk by what he spent from yeer to yeer upon my education, that in 6 yeers time it was plainly doubled, wch himself took great notice of, and spake of it to myself and others, to ye praise of God, wth Admiration and thankfulness. And after he had lived under great & sore affliction for yᵉ space of 13 yeers a pattern of faith, patience, humility & heavenlymindedness, having done his work in my education and receivᵈ an answer to his prayers God took him to his Heavenly Rest, where he is now reaping yᵉ fruit of his Laboʳs. When I came first to yᵉ Colledge, I had indeed enjoyd yᵉ benefit of Religious & strict education, and God in his mercy & pitty kept me from scandalous sins before I came thither & after I came there, but alas I had a naughty vile heart and was acted by corrupt nature & therefore could propound no Right & noble ends to myself, but acted from self and for self. I was indeed studious & strove to outdoe my compeers, but it was for honoʳ & applause & prefermᵗ & such poor Beggarly ends. Thus I had my Ends and God had his Euds far differing from mine, yet it pleased him to Bless my studies, & to make me grow in Knowledge both in yᵉ Tongues & Inferior Arts & also in Divinity. But when I had been there about 3 yeers and a half; God in his Love & Pitty to my soul wrought a great change in me, both in heart & Life, and from that Time forward I learnt to study with God & for God. And whereas before that, I had thoughts of applying myself to yᵉ study & Practise of Physick, I wholy laid aside those thoughts, and did chuse to serve Christ in yᵉ work of yᵉ ministry if he would please to fit me for it & to accept of my service in that great work.

NO. II.

EDITIONS OF WIGGLESWORTH'S POEMS.

The following are the titles of such of the different editions of *The Day of Doom* and *Meat out of the Eater*, as I have been able to find. The collations will enable persons having imperfect copies of the editions collated to identify them. Those who have other editions of the author's writings or more perfect ones of these are invited to send me collations of them.

The Day of Doom.

1662. It is evident from Mr. Wigglesworth's private memoranda quoted in the memoir (*ante*, p. 66), that the first edition of this work was published in the year 1662. It consisted of eighteen hundred copies, most of which were disposed of within a year. It was probably printed at Cambridge, though it is not found in the extensive lists of books printed there which Thomas gives in his History of Printing. I have not seen nor heard of a copy of this edition, and neither of the imperfect copies of which collations are given could possibly be the first edition, for they both contain marginal references, which were not in this edition.

1666 or 1667. The only information I find about this edition is this, contained in the author's private memoranda, that it was published about four years after the first impression and that the marginal references first appeared in this edition.

1673.— The Day of Doom : | or, a | Description | Of the

Great and Last | Judgment | With | a Short Discourse | a-
bout | Eternity | — | Eccles. 12, 14. | For God shall
bring ...... it be evil | — | London, | Printed by W. G.
for *John Sims*, at the *Kings-* | *Head* at *Sweetings Alley* in
Cornhill | next House to the *Royal-Exchange*, 1673." (The
text from the Bible is printed in full).

Title 1 f.; verso blank. A Prayer unto Christ, &c., 1½
pages, sig. A.² The Day of Doom, pp. 1 to 67. Lines without heading, pp. 68 (misprinted 70) to 71. On Eternity,
pp. 72 to part of 77. Postscript, the rest of p. 77 to 88.
Vanity of Vanities, pp. 89 to 92, A³ to E¹² in 12s. On p.
67, at the end of the Day of Doom is the word " Finis,"
which is repeated at the end of the book.

It will be noticed that the name of the author is not on
the title-page. It does not occur in any part of the book.
I presume this is the *third* edition of the *Day of Doom*,
whether it was reckoned so by the American publishers of
the work or not. As it does not contain marginal references,
I suppose it was reprinted from the *first* edition, which it is
possible may have been anonymous.

The lines on pp. 70 [68], 69, 70 and 71, I do not find in
any other edition, American or English. They number
116 lines, and begin:

> " *I walk'd and did a Little* Mole-hill *view*,
>   Full peopled with a most industrious crew.

and end:

> " Christ *yet entreats, but if you will not turn*,
>   *Where grace will not convert there fire will burn.*"

I think these lines were added by the London editor or publisher, and that they are not the production of Mr. Wigglesworth.

Perfect copies of this edition are in the libraries of James Lenox, Esq., of New York and the Prince Library, Boston, and an imperfect copy is owned by Charles Deane, Esq., of Cambridge.

1701.—In the index to the volume containing the copy of which a collation marked B is given below, which index is in the handwriting of the late Thomas Walcutt. Esq., who formerly owned it, is this memorandum: "The 5th Ed., appeared 1701." Possibly this copy may be the fifth edition.

1707.—The late Frederic S. Hill, who wrote the article on Wigglesworth in Kettell's *Specimens of American Poetry* (vol. I. p. 36), states in that article that he copied the Epitaph on Wigglesworth from " the sixth edition of Wigglesworth's Poems printed in 1707." I think he is mistaken as to the date, though it is possible there may have been an edition printed this year. An edition professing to be the sixth was published in 1715.

1711.— " The | Day of Doom : | or, a | Poetical Discription [sic.] | of | The great and last Judment [sic.] | with | a short Discourse about Eterni- | ty | — | By Michael Wigglesworth Teacher of | the Church at Maldon in New Eng- | land. | — | Acts 17, 31. | Because ... the | which ... in | Righteousness ... he | hath Ordained. | Mat : 24, 30. | And ... Man | in ... of the | Earth ... man | coming ...

Power | and great Glory. | — | Newcastle upon Tyne. |
Printed by John White in the Close | 1711." 12mo.

Title 1 f. verso blank. To the Christian Reader (signed
" Michael Wigglesworth ") 4 pp. On the following work
and its Author (signed " I. M.") 2 pp. A prayer unto
Christ the Judge of the world, 1 p. on the verso of which
commences the pagination of the Day of Doom, pp. 1 to 50.
A short Discourse about Eternity, 51, which completes sig.
E. The next page is also 51 and the Discourse continues
to the middle of p. 55. A Postscript unto the Reader, p.
56 to middle of p. 67. A Song of Emptiness or Vanity, p.
68 to middle of p. 72, after which " Finis."

This collation has been made for me by Col. Joseph L.
Chester, from a copy in the British Museum. An imperfect
copy is owned by William Reed Deane, Esq., of Mansfield.

1715.— " The Day of | Doom | or | A Poetical Descrip-
tion of the | Great and Last | Judgment. | With a Short
Discourse about | Eternity | — | By Michael Wigglesworth,
A.M., Teach- | er of the Church at Maldon in N. E. | — |
The Sixth Edition, Enlarged with | scripture and marginal
Notes. | — | Act, 17, 31, Because ...... ordained | Mat. 24,
30. And then ...... Glory [both in full] | Boston : Printed
by John Allen for Benja- | min Eliot, at his Shop in King
Street, 1715." Fcp. 12mo. Sigs. B to G in 6s ; II 5 leaves.

In the Christian Reader pp. 5–10, signed Mich. Wiggles-
worth ; On the following Work, &c., 10 to part of 11, signed
J. Mitchel ; A Prayer unto Christ, the rest of 11 to 12 ;
The Day of Doom, 1 to 51 ; A Short Discourse on Eternity,

rest of 51 to 56; A Postscript, &c., 57 to part of 69; A
Song of Emptiness, rest of 69 to 72; Death Expected, &c,
73; A Farewel, &c., 74 to part of 76; A Character of the
Reverend Author Mr. Michael Wigglesworth; In a Funeral
Sermon Preached at Maldon, June 24, 1705. By the
Reverend Dr. Cotton Mather, rest of 76 to 81; Epitaph ...
Finis, 82.

1751.— "The | Day of Doom: | or, | A Poetical Descrip-
tion of the | Great and Last | Judgment. | With a short
Discourse about | Eternity. | — | By Michael Wigglesworth,
A.M., Teacher of the | Church in Maldon, New Eng-
land. | — | The Seventh Edition, Enlarged | — | With a
Recommendatory Epistle (in Verse) by the Rev. | Mr. John
Mitchel: Also Mr. Wigglesworth's Character, | by Dr.
Cotton Mather. | — | Acts 17, 31, Because, &c., Mat. 24,
30, And then, &c. [both in full] | Boston: Printed and sold
by Thomas Fleet at the | Heart and Crown in Cornhill,
1751," Fcp. 8vo. Sigs. in 4s. No pp. 3 and 4 unless an
advertisement preceding the title page is counted.

To the Christian Reader, pp. 5-9, signed Michael Wigglesworth; On the following Work and its Author, pp. 10-11,
signed J. Mitchel; A Prayer unto Christ, &c., p. 12; The
Day of Doom, pp. 13 to part of 73; A Short Discourse on
Eternity, rest of 73 to part of 79; A Postscript to the
Reader, rest of 79 to part of 92; A Song of Emptiness, rest
of 92 to part of 96; Death Expected, &c., rest of 96 to part
of 97; A Farewel to the World, rest of 97 to part of 99; Mr.
Wigglesworth's Character, by the Reverend Dr. Cotton

Mather, rest of 99 to part of 104; Epitaph ... Finis, rest of 104.

The inventory of Thomas Fleet, June 1, 1759, contains 90 copies of Day of Doom valued at 22s. 6d., that is 3d. each. They were probably in sheets.

1811.— "The | Day of Doom : | or | A Poetical Descrip-tion | of the | Great and Last Judgment | With a short discourse on | Eternity. | By Michael Wigglesworth, A.M. | Teacher of the Church at Malden, N. E. | To which is pre-fixed a Biographical Sketch | of the character of the author | Acts 17, 31, Because ... ordained. | Mat. 24, 30, And then ... Glory. | From the Sixth Boston Edition, printed in 1715. | Newburyport: Published by E. Little & Co. | 1811 | C. Norris & Co., printers." |

Title 1 f. ; verso blank. Biographical sketch, pp. 3–9, followed by a blank page. To the Christian Reader, pp. 11–15, signed by the author. On the following work and its author, pp. 16–17, signed, J. Mitchell. A Prayer to Christ, page 18 ; sig. including title page A in 9s. The Day of Doom, pp. 19 to part of 69. On Eternity the rest of p. 69 to 74. Postscript, pp. 75 to part of 85. Vanity of Vanities, the rest of p. 85 to 88. Death Expected and Welcomed, the rest of p. 88. A Farewell to the World, pp. 89 and 90. Sig. B to verso E9 in 9s.

I have seen only two copies of this edition, one belonging to James Lenox, Esq., of New York, and the other to J. Wingate Thornton, Esq., of Boston ; and have heard of no others. I have made enquiries through a friend at Newburyport among aged people and others likely to be informed on this subject, but cannot hear of a copy there or find a person who had heard of the edition previously. I had an article inserted in the *Newburyport Herald*, Nov. 26, 1869, inquiring for copies with no better result. The publishers, Messrs. Edward Little & Co., were burnt out in the "great fire" the year it was published, and probably the whole edition was burnt with the exception of a few copies. The book is not noticed or advertised in the *Newburyport Herald* during the year 1811.

1828.— "The | Day of Doom | or | a Poetical Description of the great and last | Judgment. | With a | Short Discourse about Eternity | By Michael Wigglesworth, A.M., | Teacher of the Church at Malden in N. E. | — | Acts 17, 31, Because, &c., Mat. 24, 30, And, &c., [both texts in full] | — | From the Sixth Edition, 1715. | Boston : | Charles Ewer, 141 Washington St. | 1828."

Title 1 f.; verso printer's imprint. To the Christian Reader, pp. 3–6; On the following Work, &c, 7–8, signed, J. Mitchell ; A Prayer unto Christ, p. 9 ; p. 10, blank ; The Day of Doom, 11 to 66 ; A Short Discourse on Eternity, 67 to 72 ; A Postscript, &c., 73 to part of 84 ; A Song of Emptiness, &c., 84 to part of 88 ; Death Expected, &c., rest of 88 ; A Farewell, &c., 89 to 91 ; A Character, &c., 92 to 95 ; Epitaph ... Finis, 96.

1867.— " The | Day of Doom ; | or, a | Poetical Description | of the | Great and Last | Judgment : | With other Poems. | By | Michael Wigglesworth, A.M. | Teacher

the Church at Malden in New England, | 1662. | Also, a
Memoir of the Author, Autobiog- | raphy. and Sketch of
his Funeral | Sermon by Rev. Cotton | Mather. | — | Acts
17, 30. Because ... he | will judge ... hath | ordained. |
Mat. 21, 30, And then ... Man in | Heaven ... and they | shall
see ... power | and great glory. | From the Sixth Edition,
1715. | — | New York : | American News Company. |
1867." | 18mo, Sigs., in 12s.

Title 1 f. ; verso copyright and printers. Memoir, pp. 3
to middle of 10. Autobiography, rest of p. 10 to 12. To
the Christian Reader, pp, 13 to 17, signed Michael Wigglesworth. On the following work, pp. 18 to 19, signed J.
Mitchell. A Prayer, p. 20. The Day of Doom, pp. 21 to
85, p. 86 blank. A Short Discourse on Eternity, pp. 87 to
92. A Postscript, pp. 93 to 105. P. 106 blank. Vanity
of Vanities, py. 107 to 110. Death Expected, p. 111. A
Farewell to the World, pp. 112 to 114. Character of the
Reverend Author, pp. 115 to 118. Epitaph, p. 119. Contents, p. 120.

This edition was edited by William Henry Burr, Esq., of
New York. It was reprinted from the Boston edition of
1828, compared with the London edition of 1673 and an
imperfect copy of the Boston edition of 1715. T e autobiography and the substance of the memoir were copied
from the *New England Historical and Genealogical Register*,
vol. xvii.

The following imperfect copies are in the library of the
Massachusetts Historical Society.

A.— This copy commences at p. 3, with the 8th stanza, " Ye sons of Men," &c. The Day of Doom ends on part of p. 57 ; A Short Discourse, &c., rest of 57 to 62 ; A Port-script, &c., 63 to 75 ; A Song of Emptiness, &c., 76. The rest gone. Pot 8vo, Sigs. in 8s. This is a very early copy.

B.— The copy commences : On the following Work and its Author, signed J. Mitchell, 2 pp. ; A Prayer unto Christ, 2 pp. follows with " Michael Wigglesworth " pasted on as a signature, all the pages unnumbered ; The Day of Doom, pp. 1 to 75 ; 76 p. blank ; A short Discourse, &c., pp. 74 to 84 ; A Postscript, &c., 85 to 94 ; A Song of Emptiness, &c., 76. The rest gone. Pot 8vo, Sigs. in 4s.

NOTE.— All the editions collated except those of 1673, 1711, 1751 and 1811, have marginal notes and scripture references. The verses of the *Day of Doom* are numbered, except in the 1811 edition.

Meat out of the Eater.

The composition of this work was completed in October, 1669, as will be seen by his memorandum quoted in the memoir (*ante*, p. 83). The first edition was probably published in that year or early in 1670. I have found no copy of the first three editions.

1689.— " Meat | out of the | Eater : | or | Meditations | concerning | the necessity, end, and usefulness of | Afflic-tions | unto God's children. | All tending to prepare them for | and comfort them under the | Cross. | By Michael

Wigglesworth. | The Fourth Edition | Boston ; | Printed by ,
R. P. for John Vsher, 1689."

Meat out of the Eater, with headings like 1717 ed. below,
pp. 3 to 50 ; then follows the title, recto, " Riddles ... loseth."
verso, " Riddles ... Wine," pp. 51 and 52. Light in Darknes,
pp. 53 to 91 ; Sick men's Health, 92 to 107 ; Strength in
Weakness, 108 to 120 ; Poor men's Wealth, 121 to 137 ; In
Confinement Liberty, 138 to 147 ; In Solitude good Company,
148 to 160 ; Joy in Sorrow, 161 to 179 ; Life in Death,
180 to 189 ; Heavenly Crowns, 190 to 208. This collation
was made by W. R. Deane, Esq., from a copy in the Prince
Library belonging to the Old South Church, Boston, since
deposited in the Boston City Library.

1717.— " Meat | Out of the | Eater : | or | Meditations |
Concerning the Necessity, End, | and Usefulness of | Afflic-
tions | unto | God's Children. | All tending to Prepare them
For, and | Comfort them Under the | Cross. | — | By
Michael Wigglesworth. | Corrected and Amended by the
Author | in the Year 1703. | — | The Fifth Edition | — |
Boston, Printed by J. Allen for N. Boone at the | Sign of
the Bible in *Cornhill*, 1717." Fcp. 12mo, Sigs. in 6s.

Title 1 f.; verso blank. Meat out of the Eater, pp. 3 to
34. The heading is not *Meat out of the Eater*, but " *Tolle
Crucem.*" The former, however, is the running title from
p. 4 to 34. This portion of the book consists of 10 meditations and a " Conclusion Hortatory." Title recto, " Riddles ...
loseth ;" verso, " Riddles ... Wine," as printed in the *Historical
and Genealogical Register*, vol. xvii, p. 145. Light in

Darkness, pp. 37 to 62, in 10 Songs. Sick men's Health, pp. 63 to 72, in 4 meditations. Strength in Weakness, pp. 73 to 81, in 4 songs. Poor Men's Wealth, pp. 82 to 92, in 5 meditations. In Confinement Liberty, pp. 93 to 99, in 3 songs. In Solitude Good Company, pp. 100 to 109, in 3 songs. Joy in Sorrow, pp. 110 to 123, in 5 songs. Life in Death, pp. 123 to 130, in 3 songs. Heavenly Crowns for Thorny Wreaths ... Finis, pp. 130 to 143, in songs.

1770.—" Meat | out of the Eater: | or | Meditations | concerning the Necessity, End, and | Usefulness of | Afflictions | unto | God's Children, | all tending to prepare them For, and | Comfort them Under the | Cross. | — | By Michael Wigglesworth | Corrected and amended by the Author in | the year 1703 | — | The Sixth Edition. | — | New London; Printed by T. Green | for Seth White, 1770." Size of printed page 2½ by 5 in.

The paging is consecutive from 3 to 140; the signatures are irregular some in 8s and others in 4s. Meat out of the Eater, pp. 3 to 34; Title recto " Riddles ... loseth," verso, " Riddles ... Wine; " Light, &c., 37 to foot of 62; Sick, &c., foot of 62 to 72; Strength, &c., 73 to middle of 81; Poor, &c.. mid. 81 to 92; In Confinement, &c., 93 to mid. 99; In Solitude, mid. 99 to mid. 108; Joy, &c., mid. 108 to top 121; Life, &c., top of 121 to 127; Heavenly Crowns ... Finis, 128 to 140. The copy collated belongs to George Brinley, Esq., of Hartford, Ct., who has furnished the items for this memorandum.

All the title-pages in the *Day of Doom* and *Meat out of the Eater*, except otherwise indicated have the verso blank. All the abbreviated texts of scripture in the titles are printed in full.

A pamphlet was printed in 1862, with this title : " The Church Moves. A Curiosity of Literature and Theology. Extracts from a Poem of nearly 2,000 lines, entitled The Day of Doom. By Rev. Michael Wigglesworth, A.M., Teacher of the Church of Malden, in New England. From the Sixth London Edition, 1715, Boston : Published by R. Thayer. Sold by Usher & Quinby, 37 Cornhill." No date. 16mo, pp. 16.

There was, as will be seen by the preceding list, a *Boston* edition in 1715, but probably there was no *London* edition that year. I am informed that the extracts were really reprinted from the Boston edition of 1828, which was a reprint from the Boston 1715 edition.

III.

"Catalogue of Mr. Wigglesworth's Books taken Oct. 22, 1705.

	£	s	d			£	s	d
Newman's Concord :	00	16	0	Parens in Apocalypse			01	0
The English Annot: 2 Voll:	02	0	0	Leigh's Crit; Sacra 2 Voll.			10	0
Marlorat: in Nov: Test:		14	0	} Ainsw : on ye 5 Books of {				
Moller: in Psalm ...		10	0	} Moses & the Psal: 2 Voll {			08	0
Diodat: Annot:		16	0	} Dr Preston on ye divine {				
Davenant in Coloss :		6	0	{ Essence and Attrib: {			01	0
Cooperi Thesaurus		5	0	Saint's Qualificatn			01	0
Examen Concil: Trident		12	0	Breastplate of Faith &				
Fox's Martyrol:		10	0	love ......"".....			01	0
Calv: Expos; Job		05	0	of Judas his Repentance			03	0
Calv: on Isaiah		05	0	His three Treatises			01	0
on Jerem :		06	0	Perk: Cases of Consc: ...			01	0
in Minor: Prophet :		06	0	Alexandrs Confut : Quak:			02	0
Harmon: Evangel :		06	0	Confer: between Reyn: &				
in Epistol		10	0	Hart			02	0
Two Bibles		12	0	Ferus in Joan :			02	0

	£	s	d		£	s	d
Burroughs of Gospel Worship...		02	6	Fair weather.............		:	6
Expos: on 3 Ch. of Hos:		03	0	Lubherti Opera..........		:	4
Irenicum.............		02	6	Alting Hebrcor: Resp:....		:	6
The Marrow of Eccl. Hyst: 2 Vol................		18	0	Berkringers Institut:......		01	6
				August: Confess:........		:	9
Taciti Opera............		01	0	Decennium Luctuosum....		01	4
Venning's Remains........		01	6	Cole of God's Sovereignty.		01	0
Buxt: Hebr: Gram:.......		01	0	Sin's Overthrow.........		01	6
Ramus his Geometry......		01	6	Burrough's Evil of Evils...		01	0
Balls Treat: of Faith.....		02	0	Vinc: of Christ's appearance to Judgment............		01	6
Cartwr: Harmon: Evang:..		02	0	Shep: sincere couvert.....		01	0
Moulin's Buckler of Faith.		02	0	Riverius his practice of Physick......	01	00	0
Herodian: Histor:........		01	0	Diatriba de Medicamentorii Operationibus..........		06	0
Dod & Cleaver's Sermons.		01	0	Charleton de scorbuto.....		02	0
Dod's form of Household Governmt...............		:	6	Sennert: Institut: 3 vol...		12	0
Horace		:	6	Hadriani Thesaurus......		02	0
Clark's formul: Orat:.....		:	8	Diatriba duæ Medico-Philosophicæ...............		01	6
Hebr: Bible...		06	0	Basillica Chymica.......		:	8
Mr Cotton of the Covent...		:	9	Willis de febribus........		02	0
Isocrates		:	6	Pathologiæ cerebri et nervosi generis specimen.		01	6
Norton ad Apollon:.......		01	0	Praxis Barbettiana........			
Pool's Dialogue.........		01	0	Index Materia Medica......		02	0
Farnab: Rhetor:.........		01	0	Harvai Exertatio Anatomica		01	6
Baxter's Safe Religion.....		01	0	A few pamphlets........		02	0
Flav: Saint indeed........		01	0	Barough's Method of Physick.............		03	0
Bayley of Glorifying God..		01	0	Lower's Tractibus de Corde		02	0
Mr. Iner: Math: of Remark: Prouid:.............		01	0	Culp: English Physitian...		03	0
Myst: of Isr: Salvat:..		02	0	Miracula Chymica........		01	0
Of Conversion........		01	6				
Of Providence........		01	0	Totll	16	13	0
De Signo fill: Hom:...		:	8				
Cases of Cons: of Spts.		:	8				
Of Prayer, &c		01	0				
Angelographia....		01	6				
Order of the Gospel...		01	0				

These Books were prized on the above mentioned day and yecr by,

JONATHAN PIERPONT,
AMES AUGIER."

INDEX.

SUBSCRIBERS TO THIS WORK.

(50 COPIES PRINTED.)

WILLIAM S. APPLETON, *Boston, Mass.*

BOSTON ATHENÆUM, *Boston, Mass.*

JOHN M. BRADBURY,† *Boston, Mass.*

REV. C. D. BRADLEE, *Boston, Mass.*

J. CARSON BREVOORT, *Brooklyn, N. Y.*

JOSEPH L. CHESTER, *London, Eng.*

REV. DORUS CLARKE, D.D., *Boston, Mass.*

E. N. COBURN, *Charlestown, Mass.*

JEREMIAH COLBURN, *Boston, Mass.*

D. C. COLESWORTHY, *Chelsea, Mass.*

D. P. COREY, *Malden, Mass.*

ERASTUS CORNING, *Albany, N. Y.*

ABRAM E. CUTTER, *Charlestown, Mass.*

HENRY B. DAWSON, *Morrisania, N. Y.*

JOHN WARD DEAN (3 copies), *Boston, Mass.*

* WILLIAM REED DEANE, *Mansfield, Mass.*

SAMUEL G. DRAKE, *Boston, Mass.*

REV. CALVIN DURFEE, D.D., ‡ *Williamstown, Mass.*

EVERT A. DUYCKINCK, *New York, N. Y.*

HARRY H. EDES, *Charlestown, Mass.*

E. H. GOSS, *Melrose, Mass.*

---

† Descendant of Rev. Michael Wigglesworth.

* Died June 6, 1871.

‡ Married to a descendant.

FRANCIS S. HOFFMAN, *Philadelphia, Pa.*

ALBERT H. HOYT, A.M., *Boston, Mass.*

REV. E. B. HUNTINGTON, *Stamford, Ct.*

JAMES LENOX, *New York, N. Y.*

ABIGAIL N. LITTLE,† *Newbury, Mass.*

LONG ISLAND HISTORICAL SOCIETY, *Brooklyn, N. Y.*

WILLIAM PARSONS LUNT (3 copies), *Boston, Mass.*

MERCANTILE LIBRARY ASSOCIATION, *New York, N. Y.*

J. MUNSELL (3 copies), *Albany, N. Y.*

REV. ELIAS NASON, *North Billerica, Mass.*

NEW ENGLAND HISTORIC-GENEALOGICAL SOCIETY, *Boston, Mass.*

NEW YORK STATE LIBRARY, *Albany, N. Y.*

NORTHFIELD SOCIAL LIBRARY, *Northfield, Mass.*

PUBLIC LIBRARY, *Boston, Mass.*

JOHN H. SHEPPARD, *Boston, Mass.*

CHARLES STODDARD,† *Boston, Mass.*

J. WINGATE THORNTON, *Boston, Mass.*

WILLIAM B. TRASK, *Boston, Mass.*

CHARLES W. TUTTLE, *Boston, Mass.*

J. VERNON WHITAKER, *Philadelphia, Pa.*

WILLIAM H. WHITMORE (2 copies), *Boston, Mass.*

EDWARD WIGGLESWORTH,† *Boston, Mass.*

---

† Descendants of Rev. Michael Wigglesworth.

WIGGLESWORTH'S ELEGY ON THE REV. BENJAMIN BUNKER, OF MALDEN.

[Communicated by John Ward Dean, A.M., to the N. E. His. and Gen. Register.]

THE following elegy, on the death of the Rev. Benjamin Bunker, written by the Rev. Michael Wigglesworth, is printed from the author's autograph copy, preserved among the EWER MANUSCRIPTS, vol. i. folio 8, in the library of the New-England Historic, Genealogical Society. It has twice been printed in newspapers. The first time, it was printed in the *Puritan Recorder*, Oct. 11. 1855, a religious paper of the Orthodox Congregationalist denomination, published in Boston. The copy was made by Dean Dudley, Esq., of Boston. A few years after, it was copied by Aaron Sargent, Esq., of Somerville, and printed in a Malden newspaper.

Upon the much lamented Death of that Precious
servant of Christ, M^r. Benjamin Buncker, pasto^r
of the Church at Maldon, who deceased
on the 3^d of ye 12th moneth 1669.

Mr Buncker's Character.

He was another Timothie
  That from his very youth
With holy writt, acquainted was
  And vers't ith' word of truth.
Who as he grew to riper yeers
  He also grew in Grace;
And as he drew more neer his End,
  He mended still his Pace.

He was a true Nathaniel,
  Plain-hearted Israelite,
In whom appear'd sincerity
  And not a guilefull sp'rite,
Serious in all he went about
  Doing it with his Heart,
And not content to put off Christ
  With the Eternall part.

He was most sound and Orthodox,
  A down-right honest Teacher,
And of soul-searching needfull Truths
  A zealous, painfull Preacher.
And God his pious Labours hath
  To many hearers blest,
As by themselves hath publiquely
  Been owned & confest.

He hath in few yeers learned more,
  And greater progress made
In Christianity, then some
  That thrice the time have had.
A humble, broken-hearted man
  Still vile in his own eyes
That from the feeling of his wants
  Christ's Grace did highly prize.

Still thirsting to obtain more full;
  Assurance of God's Love:
And striving to be liker Christ
  And to the Saints above.
Although he was endu'ed with Gifts
  And Graces more then many's;
Yet he himself esteemed still
  More poor & vile then any.

In fruitless, empty, vain discourse,
  He took no good content:
But when he talk't of Heav'nly things,
  That seem'd his element.
There you might see his heart, & know
  What was his greatest Pleasure,
To speak & hear concerning Christ
  Who was his onely Treasure;

His constant self-denying frame,
  To all true saints his love,
His meekness, sweetness, Innocence
  And spirit of a Dove,
Let there be graven on our hearts
  And never be forgot.
The name of precious saints shall live,
  When wicked mens shall rot.

O Maldon, Maldon thou hast long
  Enjoy'd a day of Grace;
Thou hast a precious man of God
  Possessed in this place.
But for thy sin, thou art bereft
  Of what thou did'st possess;
Oh let thy sins afflict thee more
  Then do thy wants thee press.

Great strokes, Great Anger do proclaime,
Great Anger, Greater sins. '
We first provoke,[1] before the Lord ['offend.
To punish us begins.
Good Lord awaken all our hearts
By this most solemn stroke
To search for, find oute, and forsake
Our sins that thee provoke

Awake, awake, secure hard hearts;
Do you not hear the Bell
That for your Pastours Funerall
Soundeth a dolefull Knell?
You that would never hear nor heed
Th' instructions that he gave,
Me-thinks you should awake & learn
One lesson at his Grave.

Repent, Repent, It's more then time
The Harvest's well nigh past,
And Summer ended: but thy soul
Not saved, first nor last.
The Belows they are burnt with fire,
The Instruments are gone,
But still thy Lusts are unconsumed:
Read then thy Portion;

If that the ffounder melts in vain
(Thy lusts do not decay)
God will account thee worthless Dross
Fit to be cast away.
Since words could not awaken us,
God tries what blowes can do:
He strikes us on the head, & makes
Us stagger to and fro.

Much more I might have said, but Time
Will not the same permit. ‘
Come let us put our mouths in Dust
And down in Ashes sit.
The Lord hath giv'n us Gall to drink,
And laid us in the Dust;
What shall we say? Behold we're vile,
But thou, O Lord, art just.

If this, and such like awfull strokes
Do not our hearts awaken,
Doubtless the Gospel will ere long
Be wholly from us taken.
If we repent, return to God,
Esteem his Gospel more
Improve it better: then the Lord
Hath mercies yet in store

We append to the elegy the following lines by Mr. Wigglesworth, which we print from a copy in the autograph of the author preserved in the same volume, folio 9. These papers were presented to the above society by the late Miss Charlotte Ewer, who found them among the papers of her deceased brother, Charles Ewer, Esq., the first president of the society. The handwriting shows that these lines were written at an earlier period than the elegy.

1
When as the wayes of Jesus Christ
Are counted too precise,
Not onely by some Babes or ffooles,
But also by the wise:
When men grow weary of the yoke
Of godly discipline,
And seek to burst those golden barres
Which doe their lusts confine.

2
When some within, and some without,
Kick down the Churches wall
Because the doore is found to be
Too strait to let in all:
The best can then nought else expect
But to be turned out,
Or to be trampled under foot
By the unruly rout.

3   •
When as the ffoxes and wilde Boares
Come in to dress the Vine,
The vinyard then is like to yield
But very little wine.
When as the Sheep shall with the woolves
For carnall ends comply,
If my Conjecture faile nice not
They'l slaughter get thereby.

4
When Godly men cannot agree
But differing mindes bewray
And by their fell dissensions
Shall make themselves a prey.

Then O, New England is the time
Of thy sad visitation,
And that is like to be the yeer
Of God's fierce indignation.

5
When some shall strive to serue the rest
To their own apprehensions
In things where difference might be born,
Then look for sad contentions
For those that conscientiously
From others doe dissent
Against their consciences to act,
Will never be content.

6
When of their Shepheards faithfulness
The sheep suspitious grow
Or slight & undervalue them
To who they reverence ow:
Or when the Shepheards force the sheep
Where danger doth appeare,
Then both to Shepheards and to sheep
Calamity is neere.

7
When Joshua and Zerubbabel
Are thought for carnall ends
To favour the Samaritans
By some of their best ffriends:
When such uncharitable thoughts
Make many hearts to swell:
God grant them grace to act their part,
Both warily and well.

Evert A Duyckinck

To JOEL M

1871 July 21 For 1 Memoir Wigglesworth

Received Payment,

ALBANY, Aug. 11, 1871.

You that would never hear nor heed
  Th' instructions that he gave,
Me-thinks you should awake & learn
  One lesson at his Grave.

Repent, Repent, It's more then time
  The Harvest's well nigh past,
And Summer ended: but thy soul
  Not saved, first nor last.
The Belows they are burnt with fire,
  The Instruments are gone,
But still thy Lusts are unconsumed:
  Read then thy Portion;

The Lord hath giv'n us Gall to drink,
  And laid us in the Dust:
What shall we say? Behold we're vile,
  But thou, O Lord, art just.

If this, and such like awfull strokes
  Do not our hearts awaken,
Doubtless the Gospel will ere long
  Be wholly from us taken.
If we repent, return to God,
  Esteem his Gospel more
Improve it better: then the Lord
  Hath mercies yet in store

We append to the elegy the following lines by Mr. Wigglesworth, which we print from a copy in the autograph of the author preserved in the same volume, folio 9. These papers were presented to the above society by the late Miss Charlotte Ewer, who found them among the papers of her deceased brother, Charles Ewer, Esq., the first president of the society. The handwriting shows that these lines were written at an earlier period than the elegy.

1
When as the wayes of Jesus Christ
  Are counted too precise,
Not onely by some Babes or ffooles,
  But also by the wise :
When men grow weary of the yoke
  Of godly discipline,
And seek to burst those golden barres
  Which doe their lusts confine.

2
When some within, and some without,
  Kick down the Churches wall
Because the doore is found to be
  Too strait to let in all :
The best can then nought else expect
  But to be turned out,
Or to be trampled under foot
  By the unruly rout.

3
When as the ffoxes and wilde Boares
  Come in to dress the Vine,
The vinyard then is like to yield
  But very little wine.
When as the Sheep shall with the woolves
  For carnall ends comply,
If my Conjecture faile mee not
  They'l slaughter get thereby.

4
When Godly men cannot agree
  But differing mindes bewray
And by their fell dissensions
  Shall make themselves a prey.

Then O, New England is the time
  Of thy sad visitation,
And that is like to be the yeer
  Of God's fierce indignation.

5
When some shall strive to serue the rest
  To their own apprehensions
In things where difference might be born,
  Then look for sad contentions
For those that conscientiously
  From others doe dissent
Against their consciences to act,
  Will never be content.

6
When of their Shepheards faithfulness
  The sheep suspitions grow
Or slight & undervalue them
  To who they reverence ow :
Or when the Shepheards force the sheep
  Where danger doth appeare,
Then both to Shepheards and to sheep
  Calamity is neere.

7
When Joshua and Zerubbabel
  Are thought for carnall ends
To favour the Samaritans
  By some of their best ffriends :
When such uncharitable thoughts
  Make many hearts to swell :
God grant them grace to act their part,
  Both warily and well.